THE SPINSTER'S FORTUNE

MARY KENDALL

BLOODHOUND
BOOKS

This book is dedicated to Archie K. Shipe, Jr., 1931-2020. A native born son of Washington, D.C., the setting of this tale, and an inspiration in his own right. This one's for you, Dad.

The door opened with a jolt. The uniformed attendant strode to the bedside where a figure lay, swallowed up by pillows and blankets. The patient's snowy mane of hair was just a shade off from the dirty white of the linens. At Blue Plains Home for the Indigent and Infirm, finances did not allow for fresh sheets and pillowcases as often as needed.

"How are we feeling today, missy?" the attendant barked. "Time for some more medicine?"

"Where...where am I?" The patient's faded cornflower blue eyes gazed around the room taking in the barred window with paint chipping around the frame and the single bulb hanging out of the ceiling. She heard clattering sounds in the hall followed by screams and yelling but her legs seemed stuck. They would not move for her to get up and see what was happening. It must be a hospital of some sort but the patient in the bed could not remember how she got here...

"Oh, don't play those games with me again, Blanche. You know perfectly well where you are. Blue Plains. One of the finest addresses in the city!" The last bit was said with a loud guffaw.

Blanche furrowed her brow and thought hard. Blue Plains? Blue Plains? But that was a poor house.

As the attendant rolled her one way and the other to straighten her bedding, she asked weakly, "But how did I get here?"

The woman shrugged. "Same ways most get here, I reckon," she said. "Paddy wagon or ambulance car."

Relenting some, she patted Blanche on the shoulder. "The doc will make rounds later today," she said. "You can talk to him about this. But we've already told you about it again and again, you know."

"Oh..." Blanche said. She had to figure this out. She tried to remember what had happened. Had she finished? There had been so much money left to hide. She didn't know if there had been enough time to do it justice.

CHAPTER ONE

The telegram caught Margaret's attention right away when she walked into the foyer. After removing her riding gloves, she slapped them down next to the envelope tray.

Picking up the feather-light, yellow paper, her eye caught the date stamped, 20 August 1929. Then she skimmed it for its content. It read:

```
1304 35th St, Georgetown, ransacked by
vandals. STOP
Closest relative to owner, Emily Magruder,
listed as Margaret O'Keefe. STOP
Please contact to make appropriate
arrangements. STOP
Law Offices of Stark, Wilson and Obermann
Washington, District of Columbia
```

After plopping down on a chair next to the table, Margaret sighed. Now she would have to tend to this along with all the other worries.

Her maid, Cassie, entered the hallway and her nut brown face spread its way into a smile.

"You get that telegram, ma'am?" she asked.

Margaret looked up and waved the telegram in her hand.

"Everything all right then?" Cassie asked.

She looked at Cassie. "Huh?" she said. "Oh...family problems."

Cassie turned her expression into a sorrowful one as if on cue. "I'm sorry for that, Miss Margaret. I surely am."

"Oh don't be, Cassie. It's my father's family home in Georgetown. His sisters lived there, but one died awhile back. Apparently, the other one has let the house go...Emily is her name. I guess she can't handle things anymore..."

Cassie wrung her hands and stood in an awkward stance. "Well then...you sure there's nothing I can get for you?"

"No...I'm going to lie down for a bit. Could you ask Mr. O'Keefe to come to my bedroom when he gets home?"

"Yes, ma'am."

Walking up the generous center hall staircase, Margaret's eye stopped at the framed photograph of her father on the wall. The photo had been taken when Charles Magruder was a young man at the pinnacle of his success in the horse breeding business. A self-assured air projected out from the photo which showed a handsome face, a patrician nose, dark eyes and full head of hair. The image was not too unlike her face, her nose, her eyes. She wondered what would he expect of her right now.

After all, it was due to her father that she and Keith, her husband, lived so comfortably in his showplace, Needham Forest. The old Federal-style farmhouse had been handed down from generation to generation through the Magruder line until there was no longer a Magruder male.

Her father, several tree branches removed, had stepped in.

At first, he made inroads with the maiden aunts who lived in the house by helping them with chores and later their finances. They, in turn, had allowed him to set up a race horse business utilizing the disheveled farm buildings that had not been tended to properly in years. Bit by bit, he had turned the place around until Needham Forest was on the map as an East Coast showplace for horse breeding.

It came as no surprise to anyone that the maiden aunts eventually left the whole operation to Charles. By that time, he and his young wife and two girls had already moved into the upper floors, the aunts long before vacating it to go to nursing homes. It had been home to Margaret ever since.

Keith dabbled in finance, but it was Margaret's inheritance that kept them afloat. Additionally, she had inherited her father's talent in business. They did not have children so her horses were her babies. But Keith's "dabbling" had become a problem of late along with some unfortunate choices on her part with banking on the wrong horses. Their finances were now in disarray with Keith seemingly oblivious to the potential of a dire situation.

Margaret sat down on the mauve chaise lounge in her bedroom and took off her riding outfit replacing it with a peach-colored peignoir over her underclothes. She moved over to her vanity and sat in front of its mirror. As she took several minutes to brush the tangles from her dark bob-length mane, her mind began to let go of financial woes and ancient aunts.

Margaret hadn't realized she had drifted off until Keith opened the door of the bedroom and it banged against the wall.

She jerked up into a seated position.

"Oh...Keith. I must have dozed off."

He walked over to the mirror and began pulling his tie loose. "Tiresome day, my dove?"

"Well...yes. I got a telegram..."

He lifted one eyebrow all the while still staring at his image in the mirror. Behind on the bed, Margaret gazed at him in the mirror too. Both of them watching him before her dark eyes connected with his lighter ones.

"Daddy's family house. Apparently it's been ransacked and lawyers tracked me down as next of kin."

"Why you? Where are the sisters?" he asked, confusion in his voice.

"One died a while ago. And the other one...I really don't know where she is...I haven't seen them since...well...since that time you and I popped in to say hello."

Keith grimaced. "You mean that time we encountered those appalling conditions they lived in?"

"Yes. That time."

"How many years ago was that?" Keith asked. "It had to have been at least ten, don't you think?"

Margaret nodded and lifted herself up. "I'm going down to the barn for a bit," she said.

"Alright, my dear. Would you like me to go with you?"

Shaking her head, she headed into her dressing room and changed into her barn clothes.

The old-style barn came into view as she made her way down the rolling hill east from the house. It banked into the hill so that the stalls for the horses were on the lower level, the side not banked. The cloak of humidity from the late summer day had lifted and, as she got closer, the smells of hay, manure and horses began to fill her nose, smells that always refreshed her. A couple of neighs came from stalls. The horses could smell her human odor coming their way.

She heard a yelp and looked over to see her Russell Terrier, Oliver, running towards her. He made a good farm dog and an even better companion when she was down at the barn.

"Come on, Oliver. Let's go." The white stub of his tail wagged in response and he kept by Margaret's side.

The trainers had finished for the day and the horses rested in their stalls. Her farm manager, Leonard, sat at the office desk with a ledger in front of him. He was a familiar sight, red plaid shirt softened with age, gray hair longish at the temples, a pencil propped atop one ear.

"Hello, Leonard. How did it go today?" Margaret asked.

"Fair to middling, ma'am. Fair to middling." He closed the ledger and pushed it off to one side.

"Why don't you call it a day? It's way past quitting time, isn't it?"

Leonard gave the ledger a quick, nervous glance and nodded. "Alrighty, Mizz O'Keefe."

He made his way up from behind the desk and stood with heavily-bowed legs clod in dungarees. His years of working with horses had taken a physical toll but not a mental one. Margaret knew him to be as quick as anyone she had ever met. She put away the thought of how he had looked at the ledger.

With Oliver at her side, Margaret moved from stall to stall making sure their blankets were on, giving them rubs on their necks and occupying herself with their needs. It brought her great satisfaction to do this at the end of day. As she did so, she became aware of another scent above the usual barn odors. There was a slight aroma of cigar smoke wafting through the air. She looked about for the source. Was someone else in the barn?

She had not smelled this in the barn since... since her father had been alive. He had been a regular cigar smoker and whenever he was in the barn cigar smoke floated overhead. She made a quick survey of the area but no one was there. Shrugging it off as her imagination, she stood at Moonlight's stall, her prized Arabian, and thought about her father. He had died of a "widow-maker's" heart attack, sudden and devastating, at the relatively young age of sixty. The lifestyle of a race horse breeder had caught up to him, a daily dose of cocktails whilst entertaining clients, late nights down at the barn, the high stakes and adrenaline rushes at the auctions. The upside was that he had loved every minute of it. Her mother had soon followed him into the breach, not really knowing how to live without his larger than life presence.

Her thoughts then drifted to the last time she had seen his sisters...her aunts. It was a spring day in Georgetown, and she and Keith had taken a jaunt on the canal path along the Potomac River after dining at Chez Bonaparte's for brunch and drinking way too much champagne. It had probably been due to the champagne that she had suggested they stop to say hello to the aunts.

Keith had gone along with it having no idea how eccentric the situation might be. They had waltzed right up from the canal path onto M Street and had continued on past the little boutiques and cafes that gave Georgetown some affinity with things Parisian. Once at the intersection of Thirty-Fifth and M, Margaret looked to either side but then determined that their block was to the right not the left.

Tugging on Keith's hand, they had made their way onto the brick-lined sidewalk in front of 1304 Thirty-Fifth Street. The block was a mixed bag of townhouses and some stand-alone dwellings. It was also a blend of well-maintained and run down at the edges. The aunts' house fell into the latter category. Standing at the faded black front door with the dirty white backdrop of siding surrounding it, Margaret looked over at Keith. "Ready?" she asked.

He nodded with a dumb smile, still somewhat anesthetized by the earlier quaffing of champagne. She plucked up the brass door knocker with the ship anchor design, thunking it back onto the door a couple of times.

There was only silence from within. She tried again while Keith walked around the side of the house and peered.

"I say, my dove...could they be sunning themselves on a back patio?"

"Maybe. I'll go with you to check so as not to alarm them," Margaret said.

Both Margaret and Keith picked their way carefully through a littered side path and some overgrowth eventually reaching the rear of the house. A gate stood partially open at the rear. Keith pushed on it and they both looked in.

The yard was stuffed with various objects strangely positioned as if someone had taken pains to decorate in a weird fashion. Jutting from the rear façade of the house, there was a stepped brick patio. Several lounge chairs were haphazardly placed around various sized planters currently devoid of any plant life. And indeed two elderly ladies were perched on the loungers, each with a broad brimmed sun hat and clothed in long, dark dresses. They seemingly had not heard or noticed Margaret and Keith at the gate.

Keith purposely cleared his throat. One of the ladies looked up and over. At that point, Margaret called out and said, "Hello, aunties! It's me, Margaret. Charley's daughter..." Her voice trailed off.

Both women made slow and cautious movements up, almost feline like in their efforts. Margaret took this as an okay to move forward and, once again, dragged Keith by the hand.

Margaret could never recognize which one was which, Blanche or Emily. But, to be fair, she really had not spent much time with them. She started to chatter. "This is Keith, my husband. You didn't get a chance to meet him yet. We were in the area…" She realized she was babbling and broke off.

"It is so nice of you to come calling, my dear," one of them said.

She then turned to Keith and proffered a hand. "And a pleasure to meet you, sir."

Their group of four stood awkwardly on the patio. "We were just out here admiring all the beauty in our garden," one of the aunts said.

Keith and Margaret looked around at the jumbled yard with its mish-mash of junk. They then nodded out of politeness.

"You see," the other aunt added. "The Japanese irises are poking up over there by the fence line." A small cluster of purple buds barely poked up amongst the rabble where she pointed. "Mama preferred them to those huge, hairy bearded iris you see everywhere."

"And, of course, the scent of our lilacs wafting over is just so lovely this time of year," the first aunt said.

Margaret breathed in deep, but did not smell lilacs. "Where is the lilac bush?" she asked.

"Well, right over there, dear. You walked right past it."

A scraggly, untended bush sat by the gate to the rear of the yard. Most of the sprays that had bloomed were now brown and finished.

"Oh, of course," Margaret replied.

That aunt turned to the other one. "Well, sister, we must offer tea and biscuits, don't you agree?"

The other one (Blanche?) nodded. "Please, won't you come in?" she said, before gesturing with an open arm to the back entry screened door which hung off one of its hinges.

"Oh, we couldn't possibly intrude…"

"No, no, my dear. Of course, you must. You are family." She beamed a wide smile that was missing some teeth.

Margaret looked to Keith to ensure his agreement. Keith gave a brief nod.

They walked in single file through the tight back hall. As they continued to walk, Margaret realized the tightness had been created by stacks of newspapers that lined either side as tall as her reach. The stacks were bound with twine and pushed tight. Margaret could see some paper peeking through, yellowed and frayed with age.

Once into the center hall proper, she realized it too was diminished by stacks. Keith gave her a bewildered look. Emily or Blanche ushered them into a front parlor.

"Let's go into the drawing room, shall we?" she said. "Blanche, bring some tea and biscuits out, will you?"

Margaret made a mental note to remember which sister was which. Blanche, who nodded and headed back the way they had walked, was a couple of inches taller. Her dress was a darker tone than Emily's. At some point, the aunts had taken off their sun hats to reveal the exact same hair color and style; white with hints of a former wheaten tone underneath pulled back in low chignons at the necks where it was fastened with a silver clip.

In the drawing room, Emily gestured towards an old horsehair-stuffed Victorian sofa. When they sat down, puffs of dust flew up into the air creating motes. The shutters were halfway slit so the room was on the darker side.

Emily perched herself on the edge of a red leather wingback chair and looked, with bright eyes, between Margaret and Keith. "So...what brings the both of you to town?"

Margaret explained how the nice spring weather had encouraged them out for a Sunday drive and talked about their walk on the canal path.

Emily then turned to Keith. "And what line of work are you in, my dear?"

Keith, who had been looking around the room at the faded,

peeling wallpaper and cracked ceiling, turned to attention and replied, "I have the privilege of managing financial portfolios for some of our nation's very important men."

Margaret cringed inside. Keith could come across as so pompous at times. He had spent some time in Britain as a child and a sort of anglophile snobbery had rubbed off on him.

Emily smiled and nodded politely. "My beau, Langley, was going to pursue that line of work as well," she said. "It's a fine business in which to engage."

"Langley?" Margaret asked. She had not realized that either of the sisters had "beaus".

Blanche walked in struggling under the weight of an elaborate tea set that showed more tarnish than silver. Margaret nudged Keith who leapt up and grabbed the weight from her. He placed in down on the coffee table in front of them. Next to the tea pot was a bowl with some cookies of indeterminate age.

"Would you like me to pour, ladies?" Keith asked.

"Oh please do," replied Blanche. She seemed exhausted by her efforts and sat in the chair next to Emily. She continued. "I don't think we've used this set in twenty years. I had to dig around the cabinets to find it."

Margaret and Keith exchanged a brief look.

As Keith poured, Emily turned to Blanche. "We were just talking about Langley," she said.

"Oh?" inquired Blanche.

"Keith is involved in finance just like Langley was going to do."

"And Blackwell too."

"Yes," said Emily. "Blanche's beau, Blackwell, was also going to engage in that. I had forgotten."

There was some silence as the four of them sipped tea and chewed the brittle cookies or, in the case of Margaret and Keith, pretended to sip tea and chew the cookies. It would be impolite to ask after Blackwell and Langley even though Margaret was very curious to do so.

To break the silence, Margaret said, "So the farm is doing quite well. Daddy would be well pleased. We have had several Derby winners."

"That's wonderful, dear. Yes, your father certainly loved his horses. So strange really."

"Strange how?" asked Margaret.

Gazing thoughtfully at the cookie in her hand, Emily answered. "Well, he grew up here in the District. We never had the opportunity to be around horses or even ride them. So I always wondered where his fascination came from...."

Margaret responded, "I guess I never thought about it..."

Blanche added, "He left home so early though...really just a boy at eighteen. We didn't see much of him after that."

Keith jiggled his ankle back and forth and Margaret knew he was getting restless. She suddenly realized she didn't know how to extricate herself from the situation. She also needed to use the bathroom. "Aunt Emily, would you mind if I used your powder room? It's upstairs, isn't it?"

The aunts shared curious expressions.

"Uh...I'm so sorry my dear, but our facilities are...out of commission right now."

"Oh. Well, what do you do for..."

"We make do," Emily answered abruptly.

"When is the repair man able to come to help you?" Keith asked.

The sisters looked at each other nervously. Emily finally answered. "Soon...it will be soon."

After an awkward moment, Margaret said, "I hate to cut our visit short but I really must find..."

The sisters rose up gracefully and Blanche said, "Of course, my dear. We understand."

Margaret leaned in to give both ladies hugs. A musky odor emanated off both of them that she couldn't quite place. Keith gave both of them delicate handshakes. As they approached the front door, Emily said, "No, no dears. That door is not working right now. We must exit off the rear."

They retraced their steps back into the crowded hallway and filtered into the even tighter back hall to the hanging screened door finally emerging onto the brick patio.

The sisters stood on the patio watching their departure through the back gate. Margaret looked back and waved. Both sisters waved back.

Once back on the street, Margaret and Keith looked at each other.

Keith said to Margaret, "Blackwell and Langley?"

She shook her head knowing nothing about it.

"What a strange interlude that was, my dove."

"Yes, but right now I am in dire need of a powder room."

They walked to M Street to find a nearby restaurant where Margaret could avail herself.

Now, as she stroked Moonlight's mane, Margaret realized she had not seen or even really thought about the aunts since then. But their situation had become her situation somehow.

Margaret's attention became diverted when Oliver began a growl. While doing so, he stared with intent focus at the corner by the open doorway. "What is it, boy?"

She walked over and he looked up at her and wagged his little stub tail, distracted by her for a second, before staring back at the corner and growling low again.

"Is it a mouse?" She too stared at the corner but saw nothing.

Shrugging it off, she headed out of the barn and whistled for Oliver to come as she did so. The smell of cigar smoke still clung to her nostrils and she wondered if all the reminiscing had brought it on. She left the horses behind her in the barn and walked into the night.

CHAPTER TWO

Keith drove at a steady clip down the old Rockville Pike. The roadway, pitted with ruts, was tough to maintain in the temperamental Maryland weather. Margaret grabbed the side of her seat on one curve in particular and followed it with, "Keith, please slow down. There is plenty of time."

"Oh, so sorry, love. I lost track there...."

Keith took special pleasure from the new roadster that Margaret had recently purchased for his birthday. Baby blue in color, it was the perfect fit for him, accented by its black leather seats and two-tone trim. An extravagant gift that she somewhat regretted given the state of their finances.

"I still don't understand why this all can't be handled on the phone. Seems a shame you have to go all the way downtown."

"Believe me," Margaret replied. "I wish I didn't either but they were very hush-hush, top secret about the whole thing. I'd like to just get it done with."

She recalled speaking to the lawyer on the phone a couple days prior. He had claimed that it was imperative that she meet with him and his staff to review some important findings.

The old train station in Rockville was ten country miles

from Needham Forest. The drive transported Margaret back to times with her father taking the same trek. He had many business meetings in the city and often she would tag along. Afterwards they always ate at the Willard where her father knew all the staff and they often found themselves joining a table of men smoking cigars and sipping whiskey snifters.

At a younger age, when Margaret finished her meal of eggs Benedict on a muffin (the same order every time), she would stare at the ornate inlaid tile designs that bordered the ceiling, where the wall and ceiling met. A ribald joke or bawdy laugh would generally pull her back into the conversational flow. She had a keen interest at an early age in adult conversation and she felt sure her business acumen developed from those days.

The train station was exactly the same as when she and her father had taken it. It seemed strange to her that people could pass from life so easily and quickly but buildings stayed around longer. As a child, she had thought the station so fancy with its Victorian décor of gingerbread trim and elaborate arches above the windows within the red brick walls.

Keith found an opportune spot angled in front of the station and pulled the gear shift to park. Nimbly stepping out, he grabbed Margaret's brief from the back seat and went around to open her car door. Keith knew how to please Margaret and stay in her good graces and this was one of those things she expected from him.

What she did not expect or need from him was his accompaniment to the offices of Stark, Wilson and Obermann. She had discovered long ago that he tended to interject in a way that threw her off her game in business dealings. She did not know what they intended to lay on her but she did know that she would be better off addressing it in her own way.

Keith and Margaret stood at the platform amongst several other stragglers waiting for the 10:10. A brisk wind pushed some leaves around. Otherwise there was little movement while the wait for the train took place.

A couple of minutes after the appointed time, the vibration on the track started up and the noise of the train engine become louder as it got closer and closer. Keith leaned into Margaret giving her a perfunctory peck on her cheek and said, "Well... safe travels, my love."

Margaret took her brief from him. "Thanks, Keith," she said. "I plan on taking the six o'clock back."

He nodded and she expected him to be right there for her upon the train's return.

Margaret sat in first class and rested her head back on the cloth that covered the top cushions. She looked out the window at the countryside passing by until it changed into the denser landscape of buildings: businesses mixed with housing. Soon it became city, as Union Station got closer.

Collecting her belongings, she stood up and filed into the line, with other passengers, to disembark. Her heels gave a satisfying click on the pavement between the rails as she made her way with the others into the station area. The green glass overhead at Union Station made for interesting lighting as she walked with a purpose to the exit. Once out of the station, she looked around and saw the sign being held up in air with her name on it.

She gave the driver a nod and he helped her into the back of the Packard. "Nice trip, ma'am?" he asked, looking at her in the rear view. She nodded.

They talked no further as the car made its way through the city traffic and down into the business corridor that housed many law offices in the District. The driver pulled over to the curb and quickly came over to her side, opening her door and holding out an arm to help her out.

She gave him a smile and a thank you and headed into the Transportation Building located at the corner of Seventeenth and H Streets where it sat squatly in white.

Righting her hat, she pulled herself up tall and headed towards the elevator. The elevator man asked, "Which floor, Madame?"

"Fourth, please."

She exited out onto a richly carpeted hallway and found the door for Stark, Wilson and Obermann. When she opened it, the hostess sitting at a desk looked up inquiringly, saying, "Mrs. O'Keefe?"

"That's me."

"They are waiting for you. Please follow me."

Margaret followed the svelte hostess down another hallway until arriving at an open doorway.

She walked into the room and quickly surveyed that the meeting consisted of four men and her. Again, she wondered what could possibly merit all this attention.

"Gentlemen," she said.

One of the men stood and clasped her hand. "Mrs. O'Keefe. Such a pleasure. May I present Mr. Donoghue, Mr. Smith and Mr. Brady?" He gestured towards the other men and then added, "And I am Mr. Stark."

Margaret again wondered why four members of the law firm were in attendance.

She decided to take ownership of the situation right away. "So, gentlemen, I am honored by your presence here, but am wondering...what is this all about?"

Mr. Stark helped Margaret into a seat next to his at the head of the table. Once he positioned himself back at the head, he leaned forward on bent elbows and said, "First off, Mrs. O'Keefe, we certainly thank you for making the journey down here. Am I to understand you travelled all the way from Rockville?"

"Yes, that's right." Margaret tried to keep impatience from her voice.

"So I know you are wondering why you are here. A most unusual situation has developed with your aunt."

Margaret remained silent. He was taking his time in getting it out.

He cleared his throat and then proceeded to talk. "The house that is still in her name but on the list for District of Columbia condemnation sites has been the subject of some... shall we say...scrutiny of late."

He turned to one of his junior colleagues. "Mr. Brady will fill us in on the details."

Margaret swiveled her head in the direction of Mr. Brady. He appeared to be about her age in his late thirties and still had a full head of sandy colored hair that lent him a boyish air. He nodded at Margaret and then spoke.

"On the night of the sixth of August, detectives at the Second District were contacted by neighbors living on Thirty-Fifth Street. The neighbors had noticed a variety of suspicious persons entering the house through the back alley entrance point and a side window at different times of the day and night. Police were dispatched and caught the thieves red-handed earlier this month. It didn't take long for them to admit that there was a ring of folks who had discovered...well...discovered treasure in the house."

"Treasure?" Margaret said with surprise. "But my aunt is in the house for the infirm I thought..."

"Yes, your aunt was taken away last year after a collapse. Seemingly indigent, she has been housed at Blue Plains."

"Well...how much treasure are we talking about?"

"So far...four thousand dollars has been recovered. There have been rumors that there is more. Much more."

Margaret sat back in the chair. Wheels in her brain began to turn with rapid fire. This could solve so many of her problems. Being overdrawn at the bank. Keith's mounting debt. Purchasing some new horses to replace those that had not panned out...

She controlled her facial expression to remain neutral, not giving any of that away. "Okay...well, how did your firm become involved in all of this?" she asked.

The lead partner took over once again. "Well, a distant relative noted the story in the papers and felt that Miss Magruder would need representation. We stepped up and have become the official counsel on record. Once engaged formally, the next step was tracking down the oldest next of kin. Which is you, Mrs. O'Keefe. I believe your sister is younger than you?"

Margaret nodded. Her sister, Judith, was not only younger but estranged from any family connections. She had taken her share of the inheritance and squandered it in off Broadway play productions. Last Margaret had heard, that was where she still was. Margaret used to go up a couple of times a year to see some of the plays. Most of them were in a word outlandish but she had tried to be as supportive as possible. But it was just never enough...a burdensome history lay between the two sisters. Their father had groomed Margaret for the business and the house and in doing so created jealousy and resentment in his younger daughter.

"And there are some cousins, like the distant relative who initially contacted us, but again you are the elder. Under the laws of this jurisdiction, that means that you can be appointed executor of the estate."

"Of course, of course," she said with no hesitation. This was a lucky penny landing in her lap just when she needed it. The cigar smoke the night before was maybe a portent of this.

He paused for a moment. "Did you not see mention of this in the papers, Mrs. O'Keefe?" he asked.

"No. I had no idea."

He pressed a small stack of newspapers in her direction.

She looked down at the top one which had a front page headline: 'Spinster in house for infirm has treasure!'

She looked up at the men, taken aback. "I've been preoccupied with my horses…I haven't really been reading the papers on a regular basis."

"Well, those copies are for you. You can peruse at your leisure. In the meantime, we took the liberty of drawing up some paperwork for you to sign. Once we process the paperwork, you become basically the authority."

He then laid out the plan. They would hire a recovery team to scour the house for all the treasures and monies. Once they entered it officially on the books, Margaret would be the overseer of how it would be spent until, of course, the passing of her aunt.

"It sounds like you have done all the work to make this happen. I assume we have to negotiate your fees."

Mr. Stark raised his eyebrows. "My dear," he said. "Our fees are the customary ones for a project of this nature."

"And what would that be exactly?" Margaret asked, adding some sugar to her voice.

"The standard of twenty percent of the whole."

Without missing a beat, she responded. "Oh that is not acceptable. Let's see if we can sharpen the pencil a little."

After some wrangling back and forth, he backed down and they agreed to fifteen percent.

Margaret sat back on the cushioned chair and let a satisfied smile pass over her face. This event was turning out so much better than she had ever anticipated.

"Now there is one more thing to discuss, my dear."

"What is that?"

"Our records researchers have discovered a rather unusual anomaly."

Margaret breathed deep to keep irritation at bay. The man liked to drag things out. "Oh?" she inquired.

"Blue Plains has your aunt listed as Emily Magruder."

"That's right," Margaret said. "It got down to two surviving sisters, Blanche and Emily, and Blanche passed away a while ago. Probably eight years at least."

"Did you happen to go to the funeral?"

Somewhat abashed, Margaret had to admit that she had not. "My husband and I were very busy that time of year. In the spring is when our business..." she trailed off. It sounded like what is was...a very poor excuse.

Mr. Stark gestured to Mr. Brady, who said, "Well, it turns out that based on records we are finding...Emily actually died at that time. Not Blanche."

"What? What records?" Margaret asked.

"Cemetery records at the Oak Hill Cemetery over in Georgetown."

Margaret furrowed her brow. "Well...so who is in Blue Plains?"

"It's Blanche. She apparently assumed Emily's identity for some reason...reasons unknown. To neighbors and others, she presented herself as Emily."

"Well, for goodness sake." Margaret looked around at the men in the room who all appeared confused by the information themselves and then said, "Okay...so how does this change things?"

"Well, we have to legally change some paperwork, but other than that it will not affect things too greatly," Mr. Brady replied.

"Okay, well then..."

Mr. Stark chimed in. "But there is something that will need to happen."

"What's that?"

"Since it will be shown on record that Blanche is no longer indigent, she will no longer be able to reside at Blue Plains. You will have to make arrangements for her to be...taken care of elsewhere. In other words, a paid establishment."

Mr. Stark gave Margaret a pointed look.

"I will have to make arrangements?"

"Yes. We can certainly provide recommendations for places for you to contact...Or perhaps she can be moved to your home." Mr. Stark had a glint in his eye when he mentioned that last part or was Margaret imagining it?

"Okay. Why don't you provide me that list and we will go from there?"

"In the meantime, we will need you to accompany Mr. Brady to visit with your aunt during the competency proceedings."

Margaret felt a frisson of unease at the thought of having to go to such a place. But with financial gains uppermost in her mind, she nodded and said, "Of course. Whatever needs to be done."

Back on the train, Margaret ordered a glass of whiskey from the porter. Once it was in hand, she turned to the stack of newspapers in front of her. She had missed a lot. Not only had the Washington Star reported on the events, but it had circulated out to newspapers all over the country too. Skimming through the headlines, the story of her aunt became fleshed out.

"Spinster in poorhouse", "living in house which is falling to pieces", "recluse", and "poorhouse inmate owner of fortune". She had to agree. The shock of the story did make it newsworthy.

Chagrin washed through her along with more whiskey as she realized how she must have appeared to the lawyers; cold hearted, disinterested, no concern for family. But it wasn't like that. Not really. There was no real connection there. Her father had rarely visited his sisters himself. Even though...even though he had named both of his daughters in part after them. Margaret's middle name was Blanche; Judith's was Emily. Funny how Margaret had not really thought about that until just now with whiskey in hand. It was a tenuous connection at best.

Her father had left home at a young age and moved on. She herself barely knew her own sister anymore. She shook her head as if to shake it all off and stared out into the darkening sky from the train window.

CHAPTER THREE

EIGHTEEN MONTHS EARLIER

Blanche stirred under the mountain of blankets and felt the cold chill seep in where the blankets had moved a little. Nights like these she ached for a roaring fire. One more roaring fire in the hearth like they used to have when she was growing up. Her mind often played back over the images of when the house was filled with the entire family. Both of her parents. Her one brother. And her three sisters. Now it was just down to her. One by one they had crossed the great divide. But it did no good to dwell on that.

Time for her to get to work. The sun had set and there was just a little street light coming through the shuttered windows in her drawing room. She moved into a seated position, feeling and hearing the cracks in her old bones. She placed a tentative foot out of the blankets and, using her arm, pulled herself up to standing.

Walking across the room, her reflection glimmered in the hall mirror with the scant light available. She peered at it. Standing at a petite five foot two inches, she still had the alabaster skin that had been the envy of all the debutantes at her coming-out ball. She kept her hair in the same fashion pulled around her heart-shaped face to gather in a loose chignon at the nape of her neck. Once shiny and deeply blonde, it now lay like a matte finish on her head in white. She smiled into the reflection, a practiced smile, and one that had served her so well throughout the years.

She sometimes wondered where her youth had vanished to. Inside she didn't feel like the aged lady who looked back at her in the cracked hall mirror. She felt the same inside. Still that debutante waiting for the one dance that would change it all. A dance that had never happened. She had remained in her father's house on Thirty-Fifth Street all these years....

She looked around at the one room that she mostly occupied these days. The faded rose wallpaper had torn off in pieces at various points in the room. The mantelpiece had chipped paint. The chandelier was missing crystals and had not been lit in ages. The upstairs had been shut off after her father, Nathaniel, and her older sister, Virginia, had died and it had just been her and Emily. They had set up her father's library as a bedroom that they shared. But then Emily had died. So she had dragged her mattress to the drawing room. She couldn't face the library without Emily there. She just couldn't.

There was so much money to hide. Blanche became overwhelmed at how much. She didn't know if she had enough time left. She walked over to the buffet and pulled out a candle. Once lit, she headed over to the back corner cabinet. It had been built into the corner years ago by a carpenter friend of her father's known for his work around Georgetown. He had done it as a special favor for Nathaniel. The family stored various china pieces on the shelves above and then below had been used for larger bowls and things.

On bent knees, Blanche positioned herself in front of the lower door of the built in cabinet. Taking a deep breath, she pulled on the knob. It stuck. She pulled harder and then harder. When it finally opened, the force caused her to fall back.

Righting herself, she took the candle and looked in. The bowls were still in place nestled amongst each other. She pulled them out. Once all was out, she reached her arm as far as it would go and felt around for an indentation on the back corner seam.

Finding it, she pressed with all her might. It gave and then her hand reached a little further. Her fingers felt the smooth wood of the teak box that she knew was in there. Grabbing it by one side, she hauled the box out and placed it in front of her next to the candle dripping wax on the floor next to her leg.

She smoothed her hands over the top surface that was inlaid with rose quartz pieces. The box had been a gift from her father's uncle. And in that box the inheritance was stored, all forty thousand dollars. She had seen the box once when Emily had shown her. But they had never opened it to look at the money.

She needed the key. Oh yes, it came to her. She brought herself up to standing and walked out of the room into the hallway with the teak box tucked under one arm. Across the hallway was the door to the room that had been the library but had later become the bedroom for her and Emily. Opening the door, she peered in, candle in hand.

The bookcase straight ahead filled the top half of the wall. Three shelves up, a teacup sat by itself, seemingly providing a decoration amongst the books. Blanche had to reach up and into the cup. The key was there. Emily had mentioned often that sometimes the best course of action was the obvious one.

She sat in the office chair that was still in the room. Placing the box on her lap, she took the silver key and placed it in the lock. It caught and sprung open. In front of Blanche's eyes lay five stacks of bills. She didn't need to count it. She knew it had never been touched. If she did count, she knew it would amount to forty thousand dollars. No one in her family had spent a dime of it. She also knew what she needed to do with it next. Blanche began by peeling up one of the rows of cash. She looked at it in dismay and wondered if she could do this. There was just so much. And she was tired. But she pulled her shoulders back and then began to roll the bills into tiny little packages. Once she had a fair number of them lying in front of her, she gathered them in her gown and began to walk about.

She began in the drawing room. Placing the candle down, she looked around. Of course! She would place a tiny package behind each painting on the wall that hung down from the picture rail. She had always thought that picture rails were such a nice invention, a molding piece lower down on the wall allowing for hooks to be perched, generally positioned where the tops of the windows sat.

She began working from painting to painting, dragging a chair with her as she went. She hooked the money packages around the wires and they all stayed in place. After finishing, she stood back and looked around. No one would ever be the wiser that there was money behind the paintings. She had been clever. Emily would be proud.

She could hear the songbirds starting up outside and it struck her that her time was up. Collecting the teak box with all the money left in it, she began the tedious process of hiding it again behind the bowls in its hiding place in the corner cabinet. She put the key back in the teacup too. It was good to be consistent. And it would help her remember.

For the present, it was time for fresh air. Best to go before the sunrise, which was coming soon judging from the shadows in the room. She exited out the rear door and onto the back alley. At the end of the alley lay a metal grate that tied into a sewer line. Her father, Nathaniel, had worked as a city engineer. He had studied maps of the city's underground passages in the evenings. As a child, Blanche had been fascinated by the maps and he had absentmindedly allowed her to look at the maps over his shoulder. Even though that was contrary to city policy.

But Blanche had a photographic memory. Nobody really took note of it except for Emily. Emily would have Blanche read the newspaper and then repeat it to her rather than read it herself. Emily especially enjoyed when Blanche could repeat quotes back line by line. Blanche never forgot the tunnel maps either. When Blackwell Swann wanted her to meet him at the Healy Building one moonlit night, she knew exactly how to make that happen...

Stemming off the sewer line, there was an old tunnel that had been long established underneath city as far back as the city planners had gone. Probably all the way to L'Enfant's era. Given the way Paris was designed, it was no surprise that the earliest city planners would have incorporated tunnels into the plan for the District.

So the old tunnel weaved its way underneath Georgetown and had several exit hatches along the way. One such hatch was at the Healy Building. Blanche and her beau had secretly met at this particular spot on several moonlit nights.

She squatted down and pushed on the metal grate. It moved easily almost as if recently oiled. She would go down into the tunnels soon...but not yet.

CHAPTER FOUR

As the crow flew, Blanche's family home in Georgetown was a little under three miles from Blue Plains. It had taken Margaret a lot longer than three miles to make the trek down from Rockville. She met Mr. Brady at Union Station. He stood outside a hired car which was to take them both to Blue Plains.

He greeted her with a jaunty nod and a tip of his hat as his face creased into a smile. After exchanging pleasantries, he took one of her gloved hands and helped her into the back seat. There was a manliness about him that reminded Margaret of an erstwhile suitor from years back. He seemed familiar to her.

Once situated, they fell into an easy conversation about horses prompted by him asking about Needham Forest. They discovered that they shared a mutual interest in attending horse events. In fact, Mr. Brady had made several forays out to Poolesville northwest of Margaret's estate where horsey type events had become a mainstay of the area.

Margaret diverted the conversation to Emily...or Blanche... asking, "Has anyone gotten to the bottom of how this ludicrous mix-up happened?"

Mr. Brady paused to light up a Lucky Strike, and offered it

first to Margaret who declined. After taking a drag, he said, "Well, I took the liberty of asking around with neighbors who live on the street. A Mr. Harkins recalled that he had assisted Miss Magruder when her sister had died."

"And?" Margaret prodded.

"Yes, he claims that she was the one who told the police that she was Emily and her sister, Blanche, had died. Says he was standing right there when she said it."

"So...do we surmise she was confused?"

"I can't say for certain, Mrs. O'Keefe. These are perhaps questions for the doctors at Blue Plains."

"Of course. And I do intend to ask them about it."

Margaret stared out the window and noted that they had turned into the long drive leading up to Blue Plains, which lay on a hilltop overlooking the western side of the city. Land had been set aside years earlier and had remained untouched even as the city moved outwards and then engulfed all around the hilltop. Yet the hilltop had not been relinquished despite the politicos and land developers that may have lobbied and jockeyed for it.

The crown jewel of the hilltop was the monumental style building constructed of masonry block. Majestic in size and scope. When viewed from a distance, there was no indication of the supposed horrors that happened within its solid, fortress-like walls. That stayed under wraps. She had of course heard the stories about the place, abuse, negligence, sordid conditions, and her stomach clenched a little at the thought of now entering its front doors.

She must have inadvertently expressed her nervousness to Mr. Brady. "The lunacy proceedings should go quickly," he said in a reassuring tone.

Margaret looked at him with some horror. "Lunacy?"

"I'm sorry...that was an unfortunate choice of word. I meant competency. Competency hearings. They used to call it lunacy, but that has become an antiquated term really."

He looked at her apologetically and she looked away. Then she turned back to him. "It's okay, Mr. Brady. There is no need to sugarcoat. Let's call it what it is."

She thought if her aunt was a lunatic that's just the way it was. There was nothing she could do about that.

The driver pulled the car to the front of the building where the drive wrapped around in a U configuration. Mr. Brady got out and then opened the door for Margaret. A steep set of marble stairs rose to the entrance way. He placed one hand under her elbow as they made their way up the stairs to the entrance. At the top, there was a buzzer marked for access.

After Mr. Brady pressed it, a gong-like tone could be heard on the other side. The door opened and a disheveled orderly stuck his head out.

"Good day," Mr. Brady said with a lean in. "We are Mr. Brady and Mrs. O'Keefe. We should be on your list."

The orderly closed the door with no response. No sooner had they turned and looked at each other than the door opened back up quickly and they were ushered in. The hall in which they stood was vast and a bitter damp hung in the air. A smell of decay hit Margaret's nose straight away. They were directed straight ahead to a set of padded doors. The orderly took keys out and unlocked the doors again, gesturing them forward.

Upon entering the next hall, the smell became worse, and sounds were emanating from the closed doors along the hallway. The tiled floor was sticky and felt as though it was grabbing her high heels.

They were taken to a large room that held an examining table and medical supplies and instruments. The orderly left and closed the door behind him. Mr. Brady stuck his hands in his pockets and jangled coins. Margaret sensed that the place was affecting him as it was her. She looked at the seat of a random chair placed against the wall. There was dirt or something looking too much like dirt smeared on one edge and she decided to remain standing.

The door burst open and a doctor stepped in with two orderlies trailing behind him. He greeted both of them effusively. "Hello, hello. I'm Doctor Michaels. We'll get started in a minute."

The doctor and his staff proceeded to shuffle various papers on the counter and assemble tools of the trade.

The doctor turned back to Margaret. "Now I am to understand that you are the family member here."

"That's correct. I am Margaret O'Keefe."

"So once we make our determination you will be signing off in agreement as to Miss Magruder's competency. And this is your counsel?"

He turned in the direction of Mr. Brady. They both nodded by way of response.

"Okay. Let's bring the patient in then."

One of the orderlies left the room and shortly after there was a bang on the door. When the door was opened, a wooden wheel chair was pushed into the space with Margaret's aunt slumped over to one side of it.

Margaret held back a gasp. She barely looked alive. She stared off into the distance. The chair was pushed up to the doctor.

Speaking in a loud voice, he said, "Hi Blanche. Remember me?"

Blanche's blue eyes slowly rolled over to the doctor's face, but she said nothing. "Now, Blanche, can you tell us your full name please?"

"I'm Emily...Emily Magruder."

"Blanche..." the doctor chided. "We talked about this. What is your real name?"

She hung her head low and, after a bit of time, said, in a whisper, "Blanche Marie Magruder."

Margaret and Mr. Brady looked at each other with surprise. Margaret thought that Blanche actually did know who she was after all.

"Good. Now, what year it is?" Doctor Michaels continued.

Her head turned to the other side of the room. After some moments of silence, a whisper of a voice came out and said, "1929."

Again, Margaret looked towards Mr. Brady, who raised an eyebrow. Knowing the year also seemed a good sign she thought.

"Very good, Blanche. Now...do you see your niece in this room?"

Blanche lowered her head and then moved it like a turtle right and left. Again the whisper of a voice came out. "Lilli Lamb is not in this room."

The doctor looked up at Margaret. "Does she have a niece named Lilli Lamb?"

"Yes. Yes, she does," Margaret said with some surprise.

Funny, she had not thought about Lilli for years. Lilli was her Aunt Anna's youngest granddaughter. Her cousin, of sorts, and Blanche's great-niece.

"Can I talk to her?" Margaret mouthed to the doctor. He gestured yes with a wave of his hand.

She moved around to the front of the wheelchair and bent down. "Hi, Aunt Blanche. Do you remember me?"

Blanche's brow tightened up as she focused on Margaret's face. After some moments, she shook her head.

"Well, it's Margaret. Margaret Blanche. Charley's daughter. It's been a while..."

Margaret did not know whether to continue or not, but the

doctor interjected. "We'll continue with the protocol, Mrs. O'Keefe."

Margaret stood back up and moved aside.

"Okay. Blanche, how long have you been here?"

She did not answer the question.

There were several more rounds of this until the doctor gestured to the orderly to remove the patient. When the door opened, unearthly sounds could be heard on the hallway.

Margaret said with some alarm, "What is happening out there, Doctor?"

He had started scribbling notes and looked up from the paper. "Huh? Oh that's just sundowner's syndrome setting in. The seasons changing has them all confused."

"I have never heard of it. What is it?"

He put in pen down and explained. "In places like this, sundowner's is a common event when the evening starts to set in. Patients all became agitated by an invisible shift, an invisible turn of a screw to be poetic about it. It can create a melee of disorder, one patient feeding off the next. If not brought under control in short order, the attendants in charge have a big problem."

"Oh. Maybe that's why we hear about Blue Plains in the news sometimes..."

The doctor shrugged and then continued. "Spring especially brings it to the forefront. But usually by this time of year we don't experience it so much."

Margaret thought about that. Spring, with its promises of new life, burgeoning growth and fresh chances. The cherry blossoms usually in bloom in Washington D.C. by late March along with the daffodils heralded in the new season. It must be like a tease to people in these places...like her aunt. A shiver went up her spine as she thought about being confined in here. If she did nothing else, she would get her aunt into a better place. A less institutional place. Her father would have wanted that.

The doctor gathered his papers. "Please let's go and have a chat in my office," he said to Margaret and Mr. Brady.

Margaret took a deep breath and steeled herself to go back out into the corridor. The doctor led the way followed by Mr. Brady with Margaret close on his heels. The shrieks and groans seem amplified and filled her ears. They soon made it to the heavy casement doors that allowed them back into the entry area. The doors slammed behind them and she could hear the attendant on the other side flipping the locks over with a resounding thud.

She let her breath out not even realizing she had been holding it in all that time. Mr. Brady looked over at her and gave her a questioning look. She just nodded in response. The doctor led them to the rear of the entry foyer and opened one of the doors.

They walked into another world altogether. An expansive office, richly decorated with antiques and painted in blue hues, this appeared to be his home away from home. He gestured to the visitor chairs that were placed in front of his large mahogany desk.

Margaret sat down in the comfortable chair and a feeling of relief washed over her. The experience had been nothing less than an ordeal.

"May I offer you something to drink? Coffee, tea...perhaps some sherry?" The doctor cordially asked.

Both of them demurred and then the doctor said, "Well, I'm going to have a little nip if it's all the same to you."

He turned to the decanter behind him in the window sill and poured himself a snifter.

Before the alcohol could enter into his bloodstream,

Margaret took things in hand and said, "So...Blanche appeared to be aware of whom she is from what I could tell."

The doctor finished a sip. "Yes, yes. I have been working with her on that," he replied. "After all the confusion about her being Emily, we finally started to straighten things out."

"How did that happen? How did you not know who she was?"

He put both hands up. "You tell me. I mean, did you know which aunt she was before all this?"

Margaret looked down. "No...I...well no," she said.

Mr. Brady stepped in. "Can you take us back to how she got here?"

"Of course. She had collapsed on the street in her neighborhood and was brought here. No one in the vicinity had any knowledge of relatives and she certainly did not appear to have any financial resources given the state of the house. So this was her only option."

"When she came to consciousness, was she able to explain anything?" Mr Brady asked.

The doctor shook his head. "Not really," he said. "It took a while, and when she could talk she said she was Emily."

"So how did it finally all come out?" Margaret asked. "About her being Blanche not Emily, I mean."

"After the house was ransacked, they tracked ownership to the surviving sister. They showed up and had a cemetery record which stated Emily died eight years back. We went round and round with Blanche and then she finally admitted it."

With that, the doctor finished his drink. Margaret and Mr. Brady sat in silence.

Mr. Brady then cleared his throat. "So the results of the competency are?" he asked.

"Well, I need to pull some paperwork together and we will certainly get back to your office as soon as possible."

Margaret and Mr. Brady both nodded.

After a pause, the doctor continued. "It would help if you had a little something for me, of course."

Margaret sat still but snuck a peek at Mr. Brady. His expression was neutral but a muscle in his jaw slightly twitched.

"We do depend on donations of course to keep up the fine work we do here," the doctor added.

Mr. Brady made a point of glancing around the room, taking in all the luxury that Dr. Michaels seemed to enjoy before answering. "We'll see what we can do."

As they left the doctor's office, Margaret looked back and saw him reaching again for the decanter.

The hired car waited for them at the circle in front of the building. Once inside, Margaret turned to Mr. Brady and asked, "What do you make of all of it?"

He shook his head tersely while pulling out another Lucky Strike and said, "It's a horrid place, isn't it?"

"Yes," she said. "If nothing else happens with all of this, I need to get Blanche out of there."

"I agree."

Margaret asked a question that had been nagging her. "Mr. Brady, I neglected to ask the other day about the distant relative who made first contact with your firm. Is it Lilli Lamb?"

"Yes. Miss Lamb did alert us to Miss Magruder's plight. Do you know her well?"

"No. I mean I met her a few times maybe when she was a child."

Margaret reflected back on her limited memories of Lilli. She remembered her as a bit strange bursting into tears for no apparent reason every time they had visited. Margaret's mother had always said Lilli was a very "sensitive" child.

"So...you are your aunt's namesake?" Mr. Brady asked.

"What? Oh...you mean my middle name. I don't know that I

would call it a namesake. Maybe it was just a nod on my father's part to his sisters. He also named my sister after one of them. Emily is her middle name. Judith Emily."

"So you must have been closer at one time?"

"No, not at all. I can count on one hand how often I saw them, honestly," she answered.

"Huh…. well, I guess families are like that."

"They certainly are. They certainly are…."

Margaret's thoughts drifted off, and they rode the remainder of the trip back to Union Station, each in their own heads.

Later that night, back at Needham Forest, Margaret sat at her desk and rolled the pen in front of her back and forth. She needed to make the call. It was the right thing to do. Finally, she picked up the shiny, black receiver and pressed for a dial tone. She asked the operator to connect her to the number in New York City. While she waited, she stared at the piece of equipment in front of her: it was magic really. The fact that a wire could connect her to her sister who was located over two hundred and fifty miles north. Sheer magic. But yet magic that she rarely pressed into use. The distance between the two of them being more than just physical miles.

After some moments went by, the connection was made and the lilting tone of her sister's voice came on the line. "Hello?"

"Judith…it's me."

"Margaret? Well, for goodness sake. What a surprise."

"I know…it's been a while. There are…some things have gone on of late."

"Things?"

Margaret went on to explain the events that had transpired. "So I guess they will sort out the competency issue and we'll go from there."

"Wait...so what happened to the one I was named after? Emily?"

Margaret patiently explained again that Blanche had assumed Emily's identity for unknown reasons but Emily had passed on years ago.

"Oh. Well, that's a shame but I have to ask, Margaret. Am I affected by this in some way?"

It was so like her sister to cut to the chase and to only be concerned if it impacted her.

Attempting to hold back the irritation in her voice, Margaret answered. "I thought you may want to..."

"But I don't know that I saw them more than once or twice in my life, did I?"

"Well, the same could be said for me."

"But they didn't contact me. They contacted you, old gal."

Underlying Judith's words was the unspoken history between the two sisters. Her father had groomed Margaret for the business and the house, and in doing so, Judith had been cut out except for some financial inheritance. So that meant Margaret had to hold the bag when things came up, such as ancient aunts ending up in Blue Plains.

She took in a big breath. "Okay, Judith. Well, I'll let you know just in case..."

Judith interrupted her. "Where's the one who is still living?"

"I told you already. Blue Plains. Where I just visited her."

"Well, she's long in the tooth too. Probably can't stay on her own I suspect. Perhaps she needs to move into Needham Forest with you and Keith." Margaret noted an undertone of glee to her sister's statement.

"We'll see. I'll be in touch then, Judith."

She shook her head while placing the receiver down. There was no way to win with Judith. She would never get over her resentment and jealousy of Margaret's role in the family game.

CHAPTER FIVE

BLANCHE

She had not been able to wake Emily one cold spring morning. If only there had been a roaring fire, maybe Emily would not have....

Sitting on the drawing room floor with the teak box in her lap, Blanche thought about that time.

She stumbled onto the street out through the side window. Racing down the sidewalk, she looked frantically for anyone to help. At one of the houses further down on the other side of the street, a gardener tended to the yard.

Blanche used to know all the neighbors through the typical interactions over the years which lent a certain comfort. But after all three beaus had perished in the war, the family closed ranks as the disappointed sisters (Virginia, Emily and Blanche) became spinsters instead of brides. There should not have been a feeling of shame involved, but somehow there was. In time, people moved away or died on the street until it was finally down to not knowing any of the people around her. Except Emily of course.

Blanche came to an abrupt stop. "Please, please," she said to the gardener. "I need help."

He looked at her and held his rake mid-air. "What is it, ma'am?"

"My sister...she's, she's...."

The master of the house came out front upon hearing all the commotion. Hands on both hips, he stood on his stoop and looked over at Blanche and the gardener. "Gerald, what's all the fuss? Why aren't you working?"

"Sir, this lady here says she's got a problem with her sister."

"I'll handle this. Get back to work."

The man walked out to where Blanche stood stricken, wringing her hands on the sidewalk. "Why don't you take me to your sister, ma'am?"

Blanche hurried back to 1304 Thirty-Fifth in a daze with the man holding up one of her elbows. Once in front of the house, the man made towards the door, but Blanche pulled on his arm and took him to the side window.

"Huh...what is this all about?" Saying nothing, she climbed in the window and he had no choice but to follow suit.

After being inside a couple of minutes, he told Blanche to wait there. He scrambled out of the window, ripping his waistcoat in the process, and hurriedly made his way to the corner where there was a fire department.

In short order, a number of people showed up and the front door was removed from its hinges. Blanche covered her ears and moaned at the splintering sound of the crowbar jerking on the wood.

Neighbors began to gather in little huddles along Thirty-Fifth Street as men worked to remove Emily from the house. There were whispers behind held up hands over faces. There were shocked expressions. The man who had helped Blanche placed hands under his suspenders and puffed up his chest.

Holding court at his end of the street while explaining the horrors he had witnessed inside the sisters' house. All shook their heads in dismay wondering how it could have gone on right under their very noses.

After the dust had settled and the emergency services had cleared out, several officials were left on the sidewalk scratching their heads and conjecturing about what to do with the lady left inside. They collectively stared at the gaping hole that had been the front door and the rest of the house that literally was coming off in pieces.

Finally one gentleman walked in through the front. Within several minutes, he was back on the street holding his head. Blanche poked her head out and yelled at all of them. "Leave me be. You won't dare get your hands on this house. This is all I have left."

Neighbors watching on the street gasped and reeled back. What would happen to the old lady in 1304 Thirty-Fifth Street? When there had been two in the house, they had just assumed they were okay, watching over each other. But now one alone?

Inside the house, Blanche placed her back on the wall and shook with fear. When they had circled around her, peppering her with questions, it seemed easier to tell them it was herself that died rather than Emily. Because, in a way, Blanche did die too.

When the ragman came to the rear door several days later, he said, "How you keeping today, Miss Emily?"

She looked up, startled for just a second before remembering, yes, she was Emily.

It would be better to be Emily now. She was the one who knew how to do things. Blanche just followed along. Emily was, after all, the big sister. Being Emily now would get her through and help her to do the next things.

She could only be expected to do so much though. The house kept falling down in bits around her. The real Emily would have done something but Blanche just...didn't.

After working for several hours in the dimly lit room, Blanche heard the Holy Trinity church bells ring midnight a block away. She lifted up the screen from the drawing room window and deftly hoisted herself up and out. Out on the other side, she pulled the screen back down and wiped her hands together to remove the dust. Looking up, she hurried her way to the back alley and then stopped to listen. The city was still with the exception of the occasional rumble of an automobile in the distance.

Her midnight prowl began. Keeping away from the gas lit street lamps, she scurried along the edges of the alley and made it out to M Street. This time of night, the city was all hers and hers alone, but she didn't take chances unless she had to.

The nights out on the streets kept her young. She had nary an arthritic bone in her body which allowed her to leap from her screened window and other places as well. She also walked the many miles she walked with alacrity.

The campus of Georgetown University called to her like a siren song on many nights. The Healy Building stood solid front and center. It took her back to her finest hours. The time she had spent with her dashing sweetheart, Blackwell Swann. Blackwell had come up from the state of Virginia to attend Georgetown. Blanche, newly turned eighteen, had met him at one of the debutante events. Theirs had been a special connection never found in another.

In the end, however, his allegiance to the state of Virginia had trumped his affections for Blanche when he had been called to serve the Confederacy. The Battle of the Wilderness in Virginia had been his undoing.

Blanche had felt a pain in her gut all day on the day he had fallen, not knowing at the time to what the pain was due. A couple of days later, the posting on the Healey Building had his name on the list of those soldiers who had died.

Her sister, Emily, had stood with her when reading the rollcall. Her voice had faltered as she spoke and said, "Black.... Blackwell Swann of Yellow Branch, Virginia."

The world had gone tilted for Blanche but Emily had kept a tight grip on her arm. That day and the days to come...

CHAPTER SIX

Cassie opened the door of Needham Forest to greet Keith and Margaret before they could get a hand on the knob. Exhausted from her ordeal at Blue Plains, Margaret looked forward to a nice, long soak in the tub and a decent martini.

"Anything of note, Cassie?" Margaret asked, weariness in her voice.

"Yes, ma'am. I put all your mails on the table. But also there been a lady calling here saying she your kin and she need to talk to you."

"Who is she?" Margaret asked.

"She say her name is Lilli Lamb. Jes like a baby sheep I reckon." Cassie's face broke into a smile.

There was Lilli Lamb popping up again. "Huh. I wonder what she wants."

"She says to tell you she made a reservation at the White Peacock Tea Room off of Dupont Circle for tomorrow at noon."

"Well...how presumptuous of her," Margaret said, turning to look at Keith.

He shrugged his shoulders.

"Is this another family member?"

"Yes...she...well, she's a cousin of some sort or another."

"I hope she's not trying to make waves with the receiving and all that...."

"I don't know. But I guess I'll go and find out."

If for no other reason than idle curiosity and a distraction from everything else, Margaret had Keith drive her into the city the next day after she had slept in, recovering from the long day prior.

As they drove from the countryside into the city, the surroundings filled in with more buildings until they reached Dupont Circle. The area had peaked during the Gilded Age with fancy mansions constructed on available lots. They drove around the centerpiece of the neighborhood, its circle, and Keith parked in a space on Connecticut Avenue which had come to serve as the commercial hub, sporting stores of international repute.

The White Peacock was located a few shops down from where Keith parked. After helping Margaret step up onto the curb, Keith said, "I'll go and track down those Cubans I have been hankering for, my dove. I don't want to get in the way of 'girl talk'." He winked at her and gave a cheeky grin. She pulled a face and watched as he trotted off to a nearby cigar store.

As she approached the entrance of the White Peacock, Margaret again recalled her knowledge of Lilli. She only remembered her as a very small child, seeming sickly, and prone to those crying outbursts. But Margaret had been a teenager and largely uninterested in small children. If truth be told, she was still uninterested.

Standing at the doorway, a flood of memories came back to Margaret as she was reminded of days past when she and her mother would take shopping excursions to the District, eventually ending up for some repast at just such a place. She shook her head to clear it and walked in. The tea room took the peacock theme in earnest and the walls were lavishly decorated with plumes of peacock feathers painted in wide splashes. Throughout the room, folding screens with the peacock feather motif divided the space. Rolling around in the recesses of Margaret's mind was the fact that white peacocks were connected to good luck. But she couldn't be quite sure if that was right.

The tables were filled with patrons enjoying a mid-day break from their pursuits, most likely shopping for the majority. There was a low murmur of conversation along with a faint tinkling of silver hitting china now and again.

She looked around the room, just realizing she had no idea what Lilli Lamb looked like. The maître de scurried up to her. "Madame?"

"Oh hello. I am here to meet Miss Lilli Lamb."

He put his hand forward with a flourish. "Right this way, madame."

Moving deftly to and fro between the tables, he led Margaret over to a corner table with a potted fern located between it and the table beside it. The woman seated there looked up expectedly.

Margaret held out her hand. "Lilli?"

Taking it, she responded. "Yes, yes. Hello, Margaret. I'd recognize you anywhere."

Margaret wished she could say the same, but Lilli bore little resemblance to the child she remembered. She carried a substantial amount of weight which she had attempted to harness into a too tight dress. Her face was mottled with some sort of skin affliction that made for puffiness. The powder to mask it did no good and seemed to lay on the surface like a sheet. Her eyes were small and beady in the doughy face.

Lilli continued. "Please have a seat...so nice of you to join me."

"Well, fortunately I had an opening today...." Margaret replied, letting it go unsaid that Lilli's short notice had not been appreciated.

"I went ahead and took the liberty of ordering a pot of Darjeeling and some crumpets. Darjeeling is all the rage with the girls in my office right now." Lilli finished the thought with a stilted laugh.

Margaret murmured her thanks and poured some tea for herself from a flow blue china tea pot.

Lilli paused while Margaret poured her tea and stirred some sugar cubes in, and then began to speak again. "Well, I'm just sick about Aunt Blanche. Just sick. Ever since I heard the news."

Margaret nodded . "How did you hear about it anyway?" she said.

Lilli gave a little grimace. "The newspaper clippings, if you can believe it," she said. "Then I contacted Stark, Wilson and Obermann right away."

Margaret paused for a moment. "Why?" she said.

Lilli, a bit flustered, replied. "Well, someone had to step in and take care of our aunt's interests, don't you think?"

"Had you ever visited her at Blue Plains?"

Lilli shifted her eyes, clearly uncomfortable, and said, "Well, no. I hadn't the chance to yet...so busy with my job. The boss has selected me as his right hand gal so to speak and, with the budget crunches, I've just been swamped." A measure of pride worked its way into her voice.

"It's not the most pleasant place I can tell you. But she will be moved to another facility as soon as all this is straightened out," Margaret said.

"Yes...so I was wondering. How will all this be straightened out?"

Margaret went on to explain what the lawyers had done

thus far and how Margaret had been appointed the executor as the next of kin.

Lilli's face crunched into a frown and she said, "You see, this is the part I don't understand. You knew nothing about this at all. I am the one that alerted everyone so...by all rights, I should be the next of kin. Don't you agree?"

Margaret sat back again and took in all that was Lilli, wondering if the girl knew how obvious she was in her intent. Then she replied, "Well, Lilli, my understanding is that the next of kin is the person closest on a family tree. Which would be me."

"Okay but.... I am the one who visited them on a regular basis and tended to their needs."

"You did? But if that were the case, Blanche would not have ended up in Blue Plains as an indigent, right?"

Lilli sat back with a darkening expression on her face, placing palms at the edge of the table, working them back and forth against the pressed white linen.

"Margaret," she said. "I think you are thwarting me."

"Thwarting you?" Margaret said with pretend surprise. "What would I possibly be thwarting you for?"

"For the Magruder family fortune, of course!"

Margaret said nothing and sipped her tea calmly. She had encountered Lilli's type before. She was like an annoying fly on a horse. Annoying but totally manageable.

"Lilli, what is it you think you are due here?"

Lilli sputtered and then began to spout off. "All the times I took care of them...visited them...brought them things..."

"Took care of them? Blanche ended up in a poor house under the wrong name. How good of care could you have possibly lent?"

"How dare you? What gives you the right..."

Margaret stood up and pulled her gloves on. "What gives

me the right is a legal document stating that I am the next of kin. That's the way it is, Lilli." She strode out of the restaurant walking tall with the intention of never seeing Lilli Lamb again.

As she walked outside, bright sunlight hit her eyes and it took her a second to get her bearings. Despite her air of calm projected to Lilli, inside she was seething. The nerve of her! As if Margaret should just hand it all over to her.

Without really thinking about it, Margaret crossed Connecticut and headed toward the Dupont Circle Memorial Fountain. She stood in front of it and took a deep breath. Its smooth, white marble along with the lilting sounds of the water dripping settled something inside of her. It was still new enough, five years or so, that it seemed clean and fresh. She recalled reading an article about the sculptor, Daniel Chester French, who had been known for his many public monuments. Lost in her thoughts, she did not even hear Keith's approach until he was right next to her.

"Well, that was a quick visit, wasn't it? I assumed I would have plenty of time to loaf here with my Cuban in front of the fountain," Keith said.

She looked up at him from the bench where she sat then said, "I'll tell you all about it on the drive over."

"Drive over?"

"We're going to 1304 Thirty-Fifth. I need...I need to keep an eye on things I think."

Keith gave a sweeping gesture and they headed for the car.

On the drive from Dupont Circle to Georgetown, Margaret finished the story of Lilli Lamb in the tea room: "So I said to her 'I am the next of kin' and walked out. The gall of it really...."

Looking straight ahead at the road in front, Keith murmured with agreeing type sounds.

"But...she was the one to raise the alarm on this, right?" he asked.

Margaret gave a drawn out yes. "She does get credit for that I guess," she said.

"So does that mean she should be in line for receiving a bulk of this?"

Margaret threw Keith a dagger-like stare and said, "Keith, I am the next of kin. So no. She should not be in line for receiving the bulk."

"But will she rattle the cage to make it so?"

Margaret pushed a large nerve of worry aside and said abruptly, "Not a chance. She's an irritating gnat is what she is."

She felt annoyance at Keith but then realized he was really only pointing out the obvious. If it had not been for Lilli, the whole situation may have gone undetected by family members and other parties may have swooped in and landed themselves a sweet honey pot.

She cast off her worries and stared out the window as they crossed town into the edge of Georgetown. The neighborhood had a distinctive feel immediately upon crossing into it. The housing was representative of another, kinder era. The small businesses with shingles out front were comforting in their connections to the past.

Pulling onto Thirty-Fifth Street, Keith parked the roadster a good distance away from 1304. Margaret looked over at him and said, "Why are you parking so far away?"

"All that debris being tossed about. Don't want to risk any damage, do I?"

She shook her head with a wry expression. She wished he would show as much care for their finances.

Margaret and Keith approached 1304 Thirty-Fifth and then paused on the sidewalk with some amazement on their faces. The house, which had been in no great shakes when they had been there years earlier, now truly met the definition of dilapidated. The sheathing in parts was hanging off or lying on the ground. The faded green shutters that had clung tightly shut to each window space now dangled as if held by a thread. The entrance space yawned wide open with nothing on it. Glass in the windows was shattered or missing. Even the brick chimney was crumbled in parts.

Margaret nudged Keith and said, "I need your handkerchief." He fumbled in his pocket and handed it to her. She held it to her mouth, delicately coughing behind it.

Dust rose almost like puffs of clouds around the house as workmen threw things out of second floor window openings. Mr. Brady had mentioned that men had been hired to clear trash and debris from the inside so that others could enter safely.

They stuck their heads on the open entry and Margaret yelled out, "Hallo? Anybody here?"

Footsteps could be heard on the floor above. "Be right down."

Margaret recognized Mr. Brady's voice and in short order he made his appearance. In the meantime, she looked around her at the work done so far. A path had been cleared by the workers but there was still much debris and general jumble.

Mr. Brady suddenly stood in front of them, still managing to look fresh in his suit despite the dusty surroundings.

Margaret felt a warmth at the sight of him, his familiarity. "Mr. Brady...I'd like to introduce you to my husband, Keith O'Keefe."

Mr. Brady being the taller of the two leaned forward with hand extended to Keith and the two men shook hands. There was an almost imperceptible sizing up on either side. But Margaret noticed. Working with horses she was tuned in to the nuances which sometimes crossed over to humans. Males sizing each other was nothing new.

The men stepped back from one another and Mr. Brady's

gaze followed Margaret's as she looked around the room. "So...
the crew has been working for four solid days now just to get to
this point. They have orders to sift through every single item of
trash before tossing it onto the trash heaps out back," he said.

Margaret nodded.

"Any...findings as of yet?" Keith asked.

"Not much yet," Mr. Brady answered. "Just some random
gold and silver pieces. We think though that the real treasure
might be on the second level. Come on up and we'll have a
look."

Mr. Brady led the charge with Margaret and Keith
following behind as the stairs creaked with complaint. One of
the workers yelled down, "Best be mindful of that staircase,
suh."

They hurried their pace upwards to remove themselves as
quickly as possible off the stairs. All three began coughing once
at the top of the stairs. There was a landing there before
narrowing off into a hallway. The dust and stench overcame
them as they collected themselves.

Margaret moved Keith's handkerchief more firmly over her
nose and mouth, trying to suck up the scent of Keith's musky
cologne as a better alternative to the smells up there.

They all entered into the first bedroom which had faded
yellow walls and a bare bulb hanging from the ceiling, the
original fixture long gone.

"We done check the mattress and hauled it out," the worker
said to no one in particular.

Mr. Brady turned to the O'Keefe's. "Yes, I had them rip the
mattress apart with a knife but we didn't find anything. Seemed
strange as that would be considered a likely hiding place..."

A metal bed frame stood alone in the room, barren without
its mattress. In addition to the frame, what remained were stacks
of books, a bureau and wooden boxes.

It was overwhelming how many things were in the house to look through properly. Margaret said as much to Mr. Brady. He wiped a hand across his jaw and said, "Don't you worry, Mrs. O'Keefe. It will be done."

"Would it be helpful if Keith and I came as receivers?"

Mr. Brady tilted his head and thought about it while Keith shot Margaret a questioning look.

"And could you explain to my husband what a receiver actually is?" Margaret added.

"Of course, of course. As the executrix and the family representative, you are officially receiving the monetary assets of the estate. In this case, receivership is happening in bits and pieces due to the nature of the situation."

Margaret replied, "So in other words it is necessary legalese to complete the proceedings?"

"You could say that."

Margaret looked at Keith to gauge his reaction. He gave a nonchalant shrug. She turned to Mr. Brady and said, "So what do you think? Keith and I can be available tomorrow."

"I don't see why there would be any objection...it is really dirty work though. You realize that?"

"Oh yes. My eyes are wide open right now. But I'd like to contribute to this."

Mr. Brady nodded and they began to make their way back down the stairs. In the drawing room, Keith asked, "So who have played the role of receivers thus far, my good man?"

As Mr. Brady answered Keith and explained more what had been done in their absence, Margaret began to study the room. A sideboard had been left standing against one wall. Corner cupboards were still in place too. They had all been gone through thoroughly as indicated by the open doors and blank insides. Funny she hadn't noticed the paintings before. Several still hung on the walls attached to an old fashioned picture rail.

She hadn't seen one of those in forever. She wandered over to examine the paintings with a better eye. All pastoral scenes of somber colors but rich detail.

Mr. Brady cut himself off from what he was saying to Keith and said to Margaret, "We haven't had time yet but we are going to have an art appraiser take a look at them."

"Hmm," Margaret murmured in response.

The men were silent behind her. She turned around suddenly. "Keith," she said. "Come help me lift one of these up."

The two men looked at each other and then Keith came over to Margaret.

"Is this one of your strange hunches, my dear?"

"Maybe."

Mr. Brady had walked over behind them with arms akimbo.

Lifting the painting off the wall on the count of three, they then placed it on the floor on its bottom edge. Margaret squatted as best she could in her skirt and peered at the back of the painting.

"Look," she said to the men. "Is that..."

They all studied what appeared to be bills rolled around the wire used to hang the pictures up.

Mr. Brady shook his head in disbelief. "Who would have thought?"

Keith looked at Margaret with admiration and said, "Wonderful, my dear!"

"I think you've uncovered a sizeable amount of treasure here, Mrs. O'Keefe," Mr. Brady said.

The unknown, of course, was how many paintings had been already removed by looters or others.

CHAPTER SEVEN

BLANCHE

Blanche had heard people talking outside her front window referring to her as 'that old spinster who lives inside there'. Spinster. She had mused afterwards about the strange word. But after so many years in her present condition since Blackwell Swann's unfortunate demise, she had to accept that she was, indeed, someone in that category. Emily had been too. So had Virginia.

As a child, she had never considered the possibility of being unmarried. In fact, that had seemed an impossibility. Yet time had worn on, and here she sat. She and her sisters had never discussed it. It was the situation in which they inhabited.

She sighed now and remembered that she had work to do. Where to hide more of the money was always the question on her mind. As the sun set, Blanche puttered around the kitchen, moving boxes around, looking for... she didn't know what. Back in one of the corners she saw a box filled with old, used, Eight O'Clock coffee cans in it. Why had they saved so many of them? She couldn't remember now what they were going to use them for.

She *did* remember, however, why they drank that particular

coffee. Her father felt strongly that the Great American Atlantic and Pacific Tea Company, the manufacturers of that coffee brand, needed their support. He had somehow tied that loyalty into ideas of nationalism and the greatness of their country. Doing his part, in other words. Blanche had never really understood the connection but after his passing they had continued to purchase only that brand of coffee from their local A & P as everyone called it. Like a lot of her father's ideas, she didn't question. She just went along with it.

She scratched her head and thought about the cans. An idea came to her. She remembered another box upstairs in one of the old sleeping rooms. It was filled with sewing notions. She made the climb up the creaking staircase, one hand firmly on the railing. She had not been up in a while but it was time. Catching her breath on the landing, she made her way into the first bedroom on the right. The room was stacked with items, as all the rooms in the house were. She looked around in the bad lighting to see if she could identify the box she was thinking of. It had been a box from an orchard down in Virginia and it had been decorated on the side with the orchard's logo. There was red in it.

In short order, her eyes rested on a touch of red and she dug out the box from the space. She had been right, there was a bag of stuffing in the box that was supposed to be for pillows or quilts but had never been used. Just the thing she needed. She had one coffee can that she had brought up with her. She began to stuff the can.

Taking the walk back to the downstairs, she took the teak box from its hiding place and got more bills out. Furling them as she had done with the others, she then pushed the cylindrical packages, one at a time, into the stuffing in the can. There! That had been a good place.

Random thoughts filled her head as she finished up her task.

She thought about those crude men who had come to her door one day, banging loudly. When she leaned out of the front window and demanded to know why they were banging so and making such a ruckus, they had the nerve to tell her that her house was a "crumbling ruins". The gall! She was just glad that Emily had not had to listen to such nonsense.

Then they had warbled on about condemnation and various laws and such. A rage had overtaken her and she didn't remember what she had told them exactly. But whatever she had said had been effective at making them leave, never to return again.

And then that horrible great niece, Lilli Lamb, always coming to check on her and Emily and then only her. Her grandmother had been Blanche's eldest sister, Anna. They had seldom seen Anna after she had married even though she lived with her husband and their children in the same city. She had been elevated to a higher social stratus upon her marriage to a Frenchman of supposed nobility leanings. Virginia and Emily had often conjectured that it was too beneath Anna to come and visit them back at her childhood home. She had made obligatory visits here and there and of course had attended their parents' funerals but...there was ill will there.

So it had been strange when Lilli Lamb had started showing up at the odd interval. Emily and Blanche would discuss her afterwards not quite understanding her sudden interest in her long lost great aunts. Until the day she had let her true motivations slip.

Blanche remembered that day well. Emily had been feeling under the weather, lounging on the couch when Lilli had knocked. Blanche had peeked out the window.

She had turned to Emily and said, "It's Lilli."

Emily had sighed and said, "Well, you must let her in. Point her to the window."

Blanche had opened the curtain fully and then gestured for Lilli to go the side of the house. Blanche moved over to the window and lifted it up just as Lilli arrived there.

"Hello aunties!" Lilli said with hearty cheer in her voice. "I've brought you some buttermilk biscuits." She held a small basket covered with a linen cloth.

She handed the basket through the window to Blanche. After setting them down, Blanche helped Lilli through the window. Lilli was on the large side and it took some doing for her to come through.

Once she was inside the room, she said, "Oh that gets me out of breath to do that. Are you sure I can't call a handy man to fix the front door for you?"

Emily and Blanche passed a look. Lilli had been trying to insert herself into their affairs for some time and they were both suspicious of it.

"No, no," Blanche answered for both of them. "We'll get to it in time."

Smoothing down her dress and arranging her hat in place, Lilli strode across the room and took a seat next to Emily on the couch.

She began to tell them a tale of how she had been on the streetcar and a very handsome man had struck up a conversation with her even though she thought it quite bold. That led into a segue on how well she was doing at the government treasury office where she worked as a stenographer.

Emily and Blanche smiled politely murmuring the appropriate ohs and ahs as necessary.

When Lilli finally wound down, there was a momentary silence. And then she said, "I would so love to see the upstairs. To see Grandmama's sleeping chamber again. I haven't been up there since I was a small child.... ." she let the sentence drift.

Emily cleared her throat. "I'm sorry, dear," she said. "It's not possible right now."

"Well, when then?"

"Why is it that you need to see it so badly, my dear?" Emily answered the question with a question. Blanche marveled at Emily's ability to handle Lilli's probings.

Lilli's beady eyes darted from sister to sister. She sighed and sat back. "Well, I have always remembered the tale Grandmama told me about a teak box that held the family jewels. She described it in such vivid detail. Before she died, she encouraged me to ask you about it. Maybe see if you would show it to me..." She arranged her facial features into a sad mask.

But Emily and Blanche did not give in to the play for sympathy if that was what it was. Emily had screwed up her face in a questioning way and said, "A teak box? Blanche, do you remember a teak box?"

Blanche shook her head.

In this way, the sisters stonewalled Lilli's attempts to finagle her way into their world. After that meeting, they had been wise to Lilli's visits and sometimes did not answer her knocks. Other times, they tolerated her visiting. She was family after all.

CHAPTER EIGHT

Mr. Brady walked back and forth in front of 1304 Thirty-Fifth as Margaret and Keith pulled up. He looked over at them and gave a nod upon their arrival.

Keith parked his roadster with care. "There he is again," he said almost under his breath.

"What?" Margaret said.

"Seems like Mr. Brady is always front and center these days."

Margaret hid a smile. It appeared Keith had taken a dislike to Mr. Brady which she had picked up on the previous day. Not his kind of man and she could have guessed as much, the two being so vastly different.

Once out of the car, they stood on the walk next to Mr. Brady and he yelled up to the second floor with one hand cupped over his mouth. "Jesse, is it safe to come in?"

Margaret looked up to see a colored man whose face was powdered with dust poke his head out. He yelled back down, "All clear, suh!"

Mr. Brady ushered them into the open front and they stood in the entry hall. Margaret noted that once again Mr. Brady was suited up in his regular office attire which made a jarring contrast to her and Keith.

They were clothed a bit more appropriately than Mr. Brady; Margaret in a casual pair of jodhpurs with a light cotton sweater atop and Keith opting for dungarees and a sharp, short sleeved madras plaid shirt.

"Sad to say today, we have just recovered a few coins here and there so far," Mr. Brady said. "Nothing like the find of yesterday. By the way, how did you think about the paintings being a place of hiding?"

Margaret shrugged. "I really don't know. It just sort of came to me," she said.

Mr. Brady chuckled and said, "Well, if anything else comes to you let us know because our job will be easier."

A young man, professionally attired, stepped into the hall and greeted them. "Hello all. We'll start up in the first bedroom. Mr. Brady, you will be the official keeper of what is being 'received' by the O'Keefes."

Mr. Brady nodded and said as an afterthought, "Thank you, Archie."

To Margaret and Keith, Mr. Brady said, "That was one of our junior associates who is assisting in the efforts here."

As they had the day prior, they made their way up the suspect stairs and Margaret breathed a sigh of relief upon getting to the landing. She lifted up a bandana she had wrapped around her neck and placed it in position over her nose and mouth. She had provided Keith with one as well and he followed her example after seeing her position it.

Mr. Brady gestured to the first bedroom with the yellow faded walls that they had seen the day before. "Okay, pick a corner," Archie, the associate, said with some enthusiasm in his voice.

Keith groaned out loud at the task in front of them while Margaret moved towards the wooden boxes.

Margaret discovered that the boxes were almost nesting style, boxes inside of boxes inside of boxes. She sifted through them and mainly found sewing materials: yarns, threads, fabrics.

Keith began to complain in his corner after perusing the stacks of books. "I've got nothing here, folks. Just a bigger pile of dust mounting up...." Margaret looked over at him as he flapped a magazine to and fro freeing more dust into the air.

She moved deeper into the boxes and eventually got to the last and smallest one. In it sat a sole Eight O'Clock coffee can with its lid tightly fastened.

Margaret felt a prickle of anticipation as she pried off the lid. Once opened, it revealed old cotton stuffing. She wrinkled her nose which had begun to itch more. Shaking the can into one of the emptied boxes, she saw something greenish float through the stuffing and then some more greenish. Picking at it carefully with her glove tipped fingers, she separated the green pieces out from the stuffings. Examining it closely, it appeared to be a tightly rolled bill almost cigar like looking. Unfurling it revealed a hundred dollar bill. She gasped and then yelled out. "I got it! I got something!"

The men came over and huddled around her. "This!" she said triumphantly holding the hundred dollar bill in the air. "And there are more here."

They all sifted through the box of stuffing and ended up with a tally of ten furled bills amounting to three hundred and fifty dollars. From that point, they were all on the alert for Eight O'Clock coffee cans.

After the excitement died down, Margaret announced that she was going to take a break. Keith trailed behind her and she led the way through the path that had been cleared to the rear door. Unlike the other time she had walked through with the sisters, the path had been greatly cleared out of the stacks of newspapers, magazines and other detritus.

Out back, standing on the concrete patio, she put a hand over her eyes and looked out into the yard. Piles of debris had been accumulating from the clean-up effort and it looked like a demolition site. Which she guessed it was.

She took in deep gulps of air as Keith lit up a cigarette next to her and propped one foot up on the walled edge of the patio. Both were quiet.

As she continued to look around the yard, she began to notice little bits of color here and there. Leftovers from the season. She remembered back to the sisters proudly showing off the flowers and plants in their yard and sure enough she now saw glimmers of what had been. Streaks of faded purple from the lilacs. Bits of yellow. Some greens fighting their way to stay. The sisters had been right. If she looked carefully enough she could see it.

Behind her stood the open gaping house that was being torn apart bit by bit. Sad that it came down to this: a house that had once been filled with people living life had now become just a shell to be brought down to its foundation. Foundations do crack so maybe not even the foundation could remain. What went wrong? What could have been done differently?

Margaret felt a sigh from deep within escape from her.

"Okay, my love?"

Keith's question brought her back to the present.

"Yes.... just thinking."

"You really seem to be attuned to how Blanche was thinking," Keith said. "Where she was hiding the money. Why is that do you think?"

"I don't know. Maybe I am starting to think like Blanche."

He raised his eyebrows.

"Say it isn't so, my dear."

"I jest somewhat but in all seriousness maybe we do need to put ourselves in her frame of mind to figure this out."

"Figure this out?"

"Yes...where the money is I mean." Margaret wondered if there were other things she needed to figure out...

Later that day, back at Needham Forest, Keith and Margaret collapsed on the drawing room couch, both feeling the effects of the day. Margaret knew they would find themselves with kinked muscles and sore hamstrings upon rising the next morning.

Keith let out a big sigh. "Do we go back tomorrow?" he asked.

Margaret looked over at him. He was sprawled out in an unKeith like fashion and had a dirt smear across one cheek. She laughed out loud.

"What?" he asked.

"Just...just...this whole situation I guess. It's very unlike us isn't it?"

He gave a rueful smile and said, "Yes, I guess so."

"But in answer to your question, yes. We are going back tomorrow."

Keith gave a resigned nod.

"I know it's taxing but we can handle a couple more days of it, don't you think?" Margaret added. She studied him as he took the last pull from his cocktail.

Smacking his lips, he placed his glass down. "Indeed, my love. Indeed we can."

CHAPTER NINE

BLANCHE

Blanche's father had specific requirements for all furnishings that came into his house. Although seemingly a female purview, Nathaniel Magruder had considered himself a connoisseur of the finer things in life. While the exterior of 1304 Thirty-Fifth Street in no way indicated anything special, the interior had brimmed over with a select décor of treasures. Nathaniel was especially proud of his elegant couches trimmed out in carved walnut woodwork with plush cushions stuffed with horsehair.

Blanche paced back and forth across the drawing room. Finally, she came to a halt and stared at the couches. With quick steps, she moved into the kitchen and then rummaged through the kitchen drawer. She walked back to the couches with a penlight and knife in hand. Before taking the first plunge with the knife, she thought of her father and how appalled he would be. Dismissing that thought, she poked holes strategically underneath the couch cushions using the penlight to guide her efforts.

After five holes were arranged haphazardly on the couch bottoms, she pushed the cigar shaped rolls deep into the horsehair stuffing.

Afterwards, tufts of horsehair floated around the room which she could make out in the dim lighting from the sun rising once again outdoors. She began to sneeze the delicate little sneeze that she had perfected as a debutante. How old must the horsehair be she wondered to herself. Older than herself of course. Maybe even older than her father....

Leaving for her evening romp, she closed the rear door and made her way through the yard riddled with glass and tin cans. After closing the gate onto the alley, she thought she heard her name being called and whipped her head back. "Fair, Fair." Shaking her head, she realized it was just the wind whistling through the newly budding branches.

Fair, the Golden Hair. No one had called her that in years. She had been nicknamed Fair the Golden Hair due to the striking flaxen hue that became even more astonishing when struck with sunlight. Her father had joked that the boys needed to shield their eyes from Blanche. Those same boys who had nicknamed her...

Her sisters had taken it in stride. Virginia, with her wren brown hair and pasty complexion. Emily a little better off with honey colored tones and better skin than Virginia. Blanche was fortunate that they had not been jealous and instead were proud to be sisters with Fair, the Golden Hair, the belle of the sixties. Or were they? She was getting confused again. Now that everyone was gone it was so hard to keep track of things, all the details.

Blanche skipped alongside Emily in her starched white pinafore and black patent leather shoes, her golden hair in ringlets encircling her face. The two sisters, lunch pails in hand, were on their way to Miss Parson's School for Girls which sat five blocks to the east of their house. Emily was responsible for getting them both there in good form and all limbs intact. Which meant she had one eye on Blanche and her white pinafore the entire way. Some trips were easier than others with a younger sister who tended towards unruliness.

Emily, being older, no longer skipped and cast an annoyed expression Blanche's way. Seeing Emily's expression, Blanche said, "Don't be such a fusspot, Ems!"

"If Miss Parson sees a mark on that smock, she'll tell Mama and then Mama will blame me. So just walk, Blanche."

Blanche answered with an exaggerated harrumph but slowed her pace to match Emily's.

"Silly Miss Parsons. Why do we care what she wants anyway?"

Emily just gave an exasperated sigh and said, "Just follow the rules, Blanche. It's not all that hard."

They soon found themselves positioned in front of the imposing brick townhouse that had four stories soaring above them. Nathaniel Magruder had chosen this school in particular for his daughters because of its offerings of the French language and elocution lessons. His two older daughters had already graduated from the institution: Anna had married a Frenchman and Virginia...Virginia resided still at the family home. The two younger girls now climbed the stairs and entered into the building with Emily glad to hand her charge over to Miss Parsons.

At the end of the day, the doors were flung open and the students made their way down the stairs. Emily waited by the stone wall bordering the property for Blanche who eventually made her way in a lackadaisical manner.

"Come on, Blanche. Put a wiggle in it."

When Blanche looked up and saw Emily, her face became wreathed into a beatific smile. Emily felt a tug at her mouth corners in response. Blanche was nothing if not equal parts charming and irritating.

Blanche began to skip along chattering to Emily all the while, filling her in on all the details of her day. "So Miss Julia told me that my voice sounds like the trilling of a bird and I told her..." and all the other details of what people said about her.

As they reached the halfway mark of their journey, Emily steeled herself when they walked by the copse of trees in the vacant lot on Prospect Street. "Blanche, shush! We are passing the trees."

Blanche looked over at the lot. "I see them! I see them!" She grabbed hold of Emily's arm almost making her off balance.

"Oh those boys are so awful. Just...quiet. Don't draw attention to yourself," she said to Blanche.

Blanche had an amused smile on her face. "I think they're funny. They are like monkeys in the jungle hanging off the trees ready to leap at us."

It was too late though. The neighborhood lads who hung about the tree limbs had already heard Blanche's chatter and they started up.

"There she is! Fair, Fair the Golden Hair!" Blanche's hair and appearance was known throughout the neighborhood and recently a certain group of boys had made it a daily mission to cat call Emily and her on their walks home from school.

Emily shivered. Blanche continued. "Emily, you can't really be afraid of boys, can you?

They began to chant louder and louder. "Fair, Fair the Golden Hair!"

Emily quickened her pace and Blanche lagged behind.

Then Emily heard Blanche say, "Hi boys!" She looked back and saw Blanche striking a pose this way and that. The horror!

And then even worse, Blanche began running towards the trees.

With a trembling voice, she yelled, "Blanche stop it! Stop it!"

Blanche did stop in her tracks and the boys' laughter floated up behind her.

Blanche walked back over to Emily but stumbled and fell on the way. The white of the pinafore became streaked with dirt on one side.

"Now look what you have done! Mama will let me have it. Will you ever listen and do the right thing?"

Blanche, after righting herself up to standing, hung her head. "Sorry, Emily," she mumbled.

Emily began a tirade. "Why do you do these things? Why are you like this? Why must you vex me so?"

In time, Blanche's nickname was shortened to just "Fair". That was what Blackwell had murmured in her ear on those moonlit nights. Oh to be Fair again for just one night. Her beauty had become a burden after Blackwell had died.

It had been a spring night like this when they had met in the tunnels for a final goodbye. They had always been guaranteed privacy down there and had taken full advantage of it once Blanche had learned to navigate from the house on Thirty-Fifth Street to the Healy Building.

Upon getting to the Healy Building, Blackwell would be waiting for her, his candle illuminating his handsome face, eyes glittering dark. He would take her hand and together they would walk deeper into the tunnels until they reached the child sized door on one of the walls.

There, behind the door, was a room. No larger than a bunk on a steamer ship but plenty of space for the two of them where Blackwell had initiated her into the enchantments of love. On the final night, before his leave taking for the war, they had stayed too long and dawn was breaking when Blanche emerged onto the back alley behind Thirty-Fifth.

She had made her way into the back door of the house, her heart breaking into pieces all the while. The house had been still but seconds after she walked in she heard stirrings in the chambers above, indicating her father was rising for the day.

She had tiptoed up to the chamber she shared with Emily. Careful not to disturb the slow, quiet breathing of sleep that Emily still enjoyed. Her body melted into her bed and she never wanted to leave it.

CHAPTER TEN

Driving down the parkway that led directly into Georgetown, Margaret felt the late summer wind whip through her hair, but smelled a hint of fall in the air. Margaret studied Keith's profile in the morning sun. He was showing some signs of his age with a few crow's feet around the eyes and some ruddiness in his cheeks that spoke of maybe too much drink. His chin had always been on the weak side which didn't get any better with age. All in all though, he retained the good looks that had always been his strong suit in life. Indeed, it was what had drawn her to him many years prior.

He sensed her scrutiny and turned to look at her. "A new day, eh?"

"It is. Strange the turns life can take sometimes, isn't it?"

"Yes," Keith said. "I would have never even remembered the aunts if this whole thing hadn't happened."

Margaret looked back at the road. Keith's comment seemed sad to her but yet she shamefully realized the same might be said for her as well.

Several hours later, Margaret landed on one of the horsehair couches in the drawing room of 1304 Thirty-Fifth, beyond caring how dirty her pants would get. She fully intended to discard her and Keith's clothes from the day anyway. After more than a half day of searching, she had struck out. As the day wore on and they moved from room to room, Margaret tried to think like Blanche. But she could not really put herself in Blanche's head. She had never really known her to start with. And then her thinking had become so twisted. Or maybe that had always been her way of thinking.

She absentmindedly ran a finger over the woven pattern on the couch. She thought how unusual that the couch was still here. In the same place as it always had been. How old must it be? How many people had sat here before her?

She realised that her father had sat here. He must have been a rambunctious little boy. She wished she could have a glimpse of him from his early years. The few photos of him as a child were posed and stilted, not giving much sense of the real person. The inner workings of a person.

Her grandparents, who had both passed on long before her birth, had also sat here. She had never known them and her father had only dropped the occasional odd comment now and again.

Her aunts, of course, had probably spent the most time on these couches. She did not remember Virginia and she could count on one hand times spent with Emily and Blanche, the most noteworthy being the day out with Keith. That day had made an indelible impression on both of them.

"Woolgathering?" Mr. Brady had quietly entered the room and looked at Margaret with a question on his face.

"Oh...I ...I guess I was."

"It's frustrating, isn't it?" he said in a companionable tone.

"It really is. Sad to say my lucky streak may have run out."

He cast a glance around and said, "Did Mr. O'Keefe leave?"

Margaret let out a sigh. "He needed some air awhile back. My suspect is that he ended up finding some liquid refreshment."

"Ah," Mr. Brady said with a curt nod.

"It's okay though. It's asking a lot of him to come down here and do all this with me..." Margaret quickly added.

Mr. Brady's expression was inscrutable, and Margaret got the sense he did not agree but would not say anything to that affect. It struck Margaret that Mr. Brady was truly a stalwart character, reliable and steady, with a strange dash of the gallant.

Keith chose that moment to crash into the open doorway. He tripped and landed, sprawled out in the foyer.

Margaret flung herself up off the couch saying, "Keith, what in the world?"

Mr. Brady lit over to where Keith lay and grabbed him under the arm. Once standing, Keith stood with hair mussed up and the unmistakable odor of alcohol wafting off of him.

"Thank you, my good man," he babbled to Mr. Brady, pushing his arm away at the same time. He turned towards Margaret and said, "Sorry, sorry, love. Lost track of time." He then brushed some debris off his shirt in a distracted manner.

Embarrassment seeped over Margaret. "Okay, let's get you home then."

"Uh...Mrs. O'Keefe, will you be okay to drive home?"

"Of course, of course." She waved Mr. Brady off as she quickly gathered her things and pulled at Keith to follow her.

"Come on, Keith," she said with gritted teeth. And looking over her shoulder, she added, "Thanks, Mr. Brady. We'll be back...soon."

Driving away from Thirty-Fifth Street, she grinded the gears of the roadster several times before making headway. Keith managed to scold Margaret despite his inebriated state.

Once back on the parkway with the gears under control, his head lolled on the passenger seat and his mouth opened, emitting soft snores.

It wasn't the first time and Margaret full well knew it wouldn't be the last. Her husband was fond of the drink. Too fond. But there were worse things she told herself. She had probably put too much pressure on him of late. She had hoped that pulling him into the affairs at 1304 Thirty-Fifth would give him a nudge in a different direction. Something to take him away from his usual ill-suited pursuits. But maybe she had thought wrong.

Keith did not emerge from the bedroom chamber the next day, and Margaret was too spent to force it. By mid-morning she made her way down to the barn to seek out the balm that always soothed her frayed nerves. Her horses. Specifically, Moonlight.

She cinched up his saddle then gave an extra tug before climbing up his jet black back. He nimbly stepped along the trail that wound its way into an open field, chomping at the bit for the freedom he knew was coming. Once in the field she loosened up on the reins and he let it rip. She clenched her thighs against the sides of the saddle and felt the breeze whip past her ears. They galloped across the open field until again it came to a wooded area and she said, "Whoa, whoa" to slow Moonlight's gait.

Back to a walk along the trail, Margaret took in the sights and smells of the old woods and thought how various ancestors tangential to her probably had been in these same woods. Her mind became clear again and eventually she pulled Moonlight around to head back to the barn.

As she lifted up and off the saddle, Leonard came out and said, "You want me to brush him down for you?"

"No thanks, Leonard. I got this."

She took her time, first removing the saddle with its now moist heat. The saddle blanket was partially stuck to the horse's sweat laden hair and she pulled it off. Then she worked on his grooming, combing, brushing and eventually tending to his hooves, taking out small pebbles that had worked in. The Arabian remained still during the proceedings allowing the grooming to take place patiently waiting for its end.

Before heading out from the barn, Margaret draped herself around his neck, feeling the pulses of his magnificent body. Tired and yet revived, she walked back to the house.

Entering the foyer, she looked over to the drawing room and saw the length of Keith along the settee. She walked into the room and found him lounging in his dressing gown with a highball in hand and his gaze down at the newspaper in front of him.

She gestured to the drink. "A bit of the hair of the dog?"

Ignoring her comment, he flicked a finger against the paper. "This right here. We need to get down to the track tomorrow and place a bet on this one. Listen to the name, Margaret." He read out loud from the paper. "Blanche's Toque."

She looked at him and said nothing. Then she took her gloves off one at a time with care.

"Not even a crack of a smile?"

She just shook her head.

"Well, I for one am going to head down to the track tomorrow and place a bet. It will take our minds off all this business down in Georgetown..." He let the thought dangle.

"No, we will not be doing that, Keith."

"Come on now, love. We deserve to kick our heels a bit."

She sat down across from him and leaned back in the chair. "There's a steeple chase event out in Poolesville. Marsden's Farm. I got the invite awhile back," she said. To herself she added no betting but of course there would be drinks. She could keep a better eye on him though.

Keith's eyes cast back down onto the newspaper as he mumbled, "As you like, my dear."

The day dawned with a touch more autumn in the air than other days. Margaret felt her spirits rise as they made the drive a half hour out into the countryside to the west. In Poolesville, they drove through the quiet burg where in the center of town sat a little red brick bank building in the middle of the street, separating the two opposing lanes of traffic. Further down, the local watering hole, the Fox and the Hound, lined up along the main drag also.

The Marsden Farm, several miles outside of town, lay among the verdant green rolling hills that eventually headed downhill to the Potomac River, the same such river that flowed in the nation's capital, indeed several blocks from the Magruder house on Thirty-Fifth Street. Sometimes it seemed to Margaret that everything was interconnected.

Keith pulled the roadster into the field on the property where all automobiles were directed. He jumped out and Margaret again took in his natty attire: houndstooth jacket and gabardine trousers, perfect for the weather and the event. She herself was not to be undone and she put her hand in Keith's and rose up showing off her lithe figure in a teal silk dress topped off with a hat with a pheasant tail feather trailing down jauntily alongside her right ear. She knew that she would meet up with a number of clients today and it was important to show her best face.

Margaret's invitation had included seating under the tent of Mr. Brock Satterfield. Finding their way over to the designated tent, they discovered a small group had already begun partaking of the feast that Mr. Satterfield had laid out. Getting closer, Margaret spotted none other than Mr. Brady.

"Mr. Brady!" she said with surprise. He turned and looked directly at her.

"Mrs. O'Keefe. What a pleasure to see you." A figure to the side of him stepped forward and touched his arm. "Oh, may I present Miss Tinsdale?"

Margaret took in Mr. Brady's companion. A slightly-built young woman with a coif of blonde bob encircling her delicate features. Really, a little china doll. She was surprised by his taste in women but fixed her face into a pleasant smile saying hello, then grabbed Keith and made introductions.

Brock Satterfield came up and welcomed all of them. If Mr. Brady's date was the china doll, Satterfield was the bull in the china shop. His short height in no way held back his large personality. The Panama hat pulled low on his forehead could not cover up the remarkably bulbous nose that projected out from underneath. A nose that was recognized far and wide amongst the horse set of the area. A rags to riches story, Brock had taken his riches later in life and dove into everything horses. He took Margaret aside by the arm saying in a low tone, "We need to meet to discuss some ideas I have, my dear."

"Is that so, Brock? Am I to assume these ideas have to do with a certain filly in my barns?"

He gave a loud guffaw then said, "You know me too well. Yes, I think I am ready to make a move in that direction."

He gave her elbow a squeeze and then released it saying, "Enjoy the event, dear."

She nodded her thanks and then rejoined Keith, Mr. Brady, and his date.

Conversation had seemed to dry up, and Keith suggested they find a seat. Once seated, he murmured to her, "Don't we get enough of Mr. Brady's company as it is these days?"

"Keith, how was I to know he was here? And there's nothing wrong with him."

Keith made an inelegant sound and said, "What did Satterfield want by the way?"

"Just business. The year old filly he's had his eye on."

Once they settled in to watch the race, Margaret's gaze drew towards Mr. Brady's broad back as he and his companion found seats. He needed to find someone a bit more interesting than Miss Tinsdale in her opinion. She went to say as much to Keith but thought better of it at the last minute.

He glanced over at her placing his spyglasses down from his eyes and said, "What is it?"

"Oh...nothing. Nothing at all."

At a break between races, Margaret stood up in her seat and stretched as much as she could. Keith looked up at her and said, "Time for an aperitif?"

She figured one could not do much damage and they ventured over to the table where a cocktail bar held a variety of liquors. A waiter donned in a red cummerbund and red bow tie asked, "May I offer you the specialty of the house, a pink grasshopper?"

Keith leaned over to Margaret and murmured, "Looks like that pink concoction that Cassie gives me for my stomach problems."

She ignored him and said, "We'll take two."

With pink grasshoppers in hand, they headed out of the tent and looked around. After a sip or two, Keith commented, "Not too bad if I do say so. Definitely better than Cassie's drink. Bottoms up love." With that, Keith raised his drink and gulped the remainder down.

"Keith..."

"What?"

"It's to be sipped not gulped."

He shrugged and headed back over to the bar.

Margaret felt the barb of irritation that she was feeling so often lately with Keith. She wandered away further from the tent and stood over the fence line. The sun glinted off of the glass that held the pink liquid. She had lost the taste for it.

She felt him come closer before he actually stood right next to her. Mr. Brady.

Keeping her gaze straight ahead, she said, "Don't miss out on the pink grasshoppers, Mr. Brady. Specialty of the house we were told."

"How is it?" he asked.

She turned to face him and said, "Fair in my estimation but maybe your date would appreciate one."

"Hmm," he responded noncommittally.

"Miss Tinsdale seems lovely. Have you been...together long?"

He shook his head. "Miss Tinsdale is Mr. Stark's niece," he said. "He asked me to accompany her today as he was called away on another matter."

"Ah," Margaret said. That made sense. Miss Tinsdale was not his kind of woman at all. She felt strangely justified... relieved even.

But he pressed the matter. "Why do you ask, Mrs. O'Keefe? Do you not think I merit someone of Miss Tinsdale's pedigree?"

He had an amused glimmer in his eye when he asked.

Without missing a beat, Margaret answered. "Maybe I think you merit someone of an even higher pedigree."

"Well, you might be underestimating Miss Tinsdale...or overestimating me." He held her gaze just a fraction longer than necessary and she looked away feeling the stirrings of something.

She gave herself a shake and said, "Well, take her a pink grasshopper in any case. She deserves that at least."

With that, Margaret headed back towards the tent feeling Mr. Brady's eyes on her back. Keith stood among a group of men and instead of walking right up to the group she stood off to one side. It was so unlike her to be rattled by a man like Mr. Brady. But then who was he really? On the surface he was just an ordinary-seeming fellow, but underneath there was more to him. It was of no matter, she told herself, as she looked over at Keith who had his head back in laughter over the mens' joke. She had Keith. She certainly did.

She inserted herself into the group and one of the men, an acquaintance of sorts, gave Margaret a hearty squeeze and asked whether they would be seeing her at the hunt next month.

"Wouldn't miss it," she said and began to engage in the idle chatter around her all the while keeping one eye on the crowd for the now strangely compelling Mr. Brady.

The day ended with a small crowd spilling over into the town of Poolesville at the one establishment available: the Fox and the Hound. As Keith and Margaret stumbled back to the roadster, it dawned on her from the herky jerkiness of Keith's driving that the drink count had gotten away from her. Margaret herself had switched from the overly sweet pink grasshopper to a couple (maybe three) crisp clean vodka tonics. But Keith had clearly surpassed her and was showing it in his sloppy driving. She made a mental note to wrangle the keys from him before they departed.

The last of the day's sunlight reflected off the tin metal roof of the Fox and the Hound and they entered into the dark foyer. Margaret blinked her eyes, adjusting to the marked change from the outdoors. The lounge area was off to the right and Brock's booming voice called out to them. "In here, O'Keefes! In here."

Making their way in, Keith announced to the people who

had already gathered, "Drinks for one and all. On me!" Margaret inwardly cringed and tried to avoid a mental tally of what this would cost Needham Forest's operating budget.

As Margaret perched herself on a tall lounge stool, a voice drifted over their way saying, "Keith O'Keefe, fancy seeing you here."

Margaret peered around Keith and took in the tall drink of water that was behind the voice.

"Oh for heaven's sake! If it isn't Laney Davis. Aren't you a sight, darling?" He paused a little too long before remembering Margaret right next to him. "Oh Margaret, you remember Laney, of course?"

"No, Keith. I don't believe so." She raised an eyebrow and both women took stock of each other.

After introductions were made, Laney drawled in a southern tinged accent to the bartender, "Henry, drinks for my friends here. What are you having?"

While Laney relayed their drink preferences to Henry the bartender, Margaret took another look at her. A tall, razor thin, dishwater blonde, she oozed the natural confidence that was too often seen in those who had never worried a second about money. Although Margaret could be wrong on that point.

As Keith and Laney chatted, Margaret idly observed others filtering into the lounge from the steeplechase event and then watched one gentleman make a beeline her way. She gave an inward groan as he got too close to her and said, "Oh Margaret I didn't get a chance to ask you about next year's plan for breeding." Harvey Atwater proceeded to demand Margaret's full and complete attention as he picked her brain on the best strategy given the market.

Somewhat fuzzy from all the drinks, she attempted to focus on Harvey's words but came up short only really paying attention to his widely spaced eyes. She wondered if anyone had ever told him his eyes were spaced too far apart. Probably not.

She soon became swept up in another conversation with a small group about the current price of a certain stallion and how opinions differed. Her glass kept magically getting refilled and food was being handed around.

Taking a break in the ladies' powder room, she realized her eyes were partially closing as she sat in a stall. She needed to leave and get back to Needham Forest. As she got herself pulled together, two women came in chattering away.

"My word, do you see how she is so shameless with Keith O'Keefe?"

Margaret went still.

"Well, he isn't doing anything to stop her, is he?" the other person said.

"You have to feel for his poor wife."

"Where is she?"

Margaret wondered where was she indeed. She debated whether to just step out and get it over with or wait them out.

The decision was made for her when one of the women said, "Oh look at the time. I've got to get back to the city..." Margaret heard the squeak of the door as the two exited still chattering all the while.

Margaret was now wide awake but splashed cold water on her face anyway. She drew her shoulders back and walked briskly back to the lounge area. She then made herself small off to the side of the room. Her eyes scanned the area until they found him. He was still right next to Laney. He must have been with her the entire time. How had Margaret lost track of him right in the same room?

As Margaret studied Keith and his cohort, she saw Keith's hand snake down behind one of her thighs. It was time to exit. Margaret marched over. They both looked up in surprise.

"Hello darling," Keith said.

"It's time to leave." Her voice was steel broaching no dissent.

Laney's mouth turned down in an almost imperceptible frown.

Keith fumbled for words and said, "Well...uh...Laney so good to see you." He rose and gave her a peck on the cheek as Margaret tugged his arm pulling him away.

Out front of the Fox and the Hound, Margaret took in a full deep breath of the night air as the small town slumbered around them. Keith lit up a cigarette.

"A little rude saying our goodbyes to Laney, don't you think?"

Margaret murmured hmm and held out her hand.

"What?" Keith asked looking at her upraised palm.

"Keys to the roadster."

"Come on now...I don't think..."

"I do."

Keith gave a big exaggerated sigh and then plopped the keys into Margaret's open palm.

The drive back to Needham Forest was a quiet one with Margaret internally debating whether to comment on Laney Davis or not. Keith too seemed to find silence the best avenue.

Margaret pulled the roadster up Needham Forest's tree-lined drive, the night around them quiet. Moonlight illuminated the house as though backlighting it. Margaret breathed in the sweet smells of home. Her home.

She realized that she would not let anyone including and maybe especially the man seated next to her to ever put all of this in jeopardy.

Once in her bed, Margaret's mind whirled around like a butter churn with scenes from the day flitting through like motion picture stills on her brain: Brock Satterfield and his nose, Miss Tinsdale and her delicate features, pink grasshoppers, Mr. Brady staring with intent, Keith's hand on Laney Davis' thigh. Finally it all stopped at those horsehair couches at 1304 Thirty-Fifth Street. Something about them niggled at her. What was it?

In her first moments of consciousness the next morning as she woke it came to her: they had torn up the mattresses upstairs to no avail but what about the couches?

With a new head of steam, Margaret wrangled Keith out of bed and got them both moving and headed down to the District. Keith, bleary eyed behind the wheel of his roadster, uttered a complaint here and there about the hour but Margaret shushed him as she continued to think about what may lay in wait at the Magruder house.

Striding through the open door, Margaret didn't bother with announcing herself to whatever workers were there. She made her way right into the drawing room where three horsehair couches sat at odd angles. With all the commotion, they had been pushed around the room and now sat in no particular order.

Keith had trailed in behind her and she turned to look at him saying, "I have an idea." She pointed at one of the horsehair couches.

He looked with some befuddlement and said, "The couches?"

"Help me lift this to the side."

"What are you thinking Margaret?"

"Just...just humor me."

They each took a side and turned the couch to one side and in the process a cloud of dust and smells from the ages rose up into the room's space. They both coughed it out.

Then they looked down at the lining that covered the bottom.

"What are those holes?" Keith asked referring to five holes which scattered about the bottom.

Margaret didn't respond to his question instead asking, "Do you have your pocket knife handy?"

He nodded and took it out of one of his dungaree pockets.

"Okay. Take it and slice into the lining here at the edge and let's lift it off."

Keith did as Margaret said. Once the lining was off, the bottom revealed the horsehair stuffing and where it had been pierced.

Margaret leaned closer in and with a careful, gloved hand reached into the center hole. She pulled out a rolled cigarillo style item much like the ones she had found in the Eight O'Clock coffee can in the bedroom above her.

"Aha! I guessed right!" she exclaimed.

Keith joined her in retrieving the booty from the other holes and they had soon accumulated five hundred more dollars.

"You've done it again, my love!" Keith declared after they had turned the couch back upright and plopped down on it.

She looked over at Keith and said, "Like I said, we need to think like Blanche."

She then looked around the room and waved a hand. "There are two more couches here."

When Mr. Brady walked in, he was greeted by the sight of Keith and Margaret sprawled on the floor next to the overturned couches.

Margaret looked up and caught his eye, saying, "Mr. Brady, you missed out on all the fun."

"I can see that. Looks like you've done it again Mrs. O'Keefe."

She waved a hand. "Please call me Margaret. And this is Keith of course."

Keith gave Robert a tip of his head.

"And I am Robert."

Bending down to their level, Robert took in the array of furled bills laid out beyond the overturned couches. Shaking his head, he said, "Astounding really."

Then he put up a finger and said, "I'll be back."

Keith and Margaret looked at each other after Robert walked out the front door.

Then Margaret said, "Well, let's stand these couches back up."

Robert returned holding a bottle of scotch and three shot glasses. He brandished it up in the air and said, "This calls for a celebratory toast I think."

"Ah good man," replied Keith with a little more life in his voice.

After a scramble for purchase, Keith and Margaret rose to standing while Robert poured for all three of them.

Keith held out his glass in front of him and swirled the amber colored liquid. "If I had to take a gander, I would say this is vintage 1920 or so. Am I right?"

Robert said, "That's sounds in the ballpark. I'm not really a connoisseur. Just like to have the stuff around for the appropriate occasion." He smiled at Margaret and lifted his glass.

She smiled back at him while Keith started to go into the merits of an older scotch as versus a young one.

When Keith wound down about the scotch, Robert asked pointedly, "Why do you think Blanche did this? Hid money like this."

Margaret walked over to the windowsill and leaned against it before answering. Then she said, "I really have no idea. But there has got to be some method to the madness I think."

Keith didn't respond and had become absorbed in staring at the label on the scotch bottle surreptitiously pouring himself another.

"Maybe you will figure out the method, Margaret, because I have yet to make any sense of it," Robert said.

"Maybe I will. But for now I think we call it a day." She stood away from the window and stretched out her arms feeling a crack in her back somewhere as she did so.

They left Robert to collect the monies for safekeeping and headed back to Needham Forest, both lulled by the motion of the car in combination with Robert's libation.

Margaret had begun to think about all the books in the house. Especially the books in the library. She didn't know why it popped into her head. All those books had been checked...but it occurred to her that she should check them again. Just in case.

Keith broke into her thoughts. "He's not a bad sort really."

"Huh?" Margaret said losing her train of thought.

"Good old Robert. Not a bad sort I said."

"Well, I never said he was a bad sort."

"He seemed a bit stiff to me the first go round. But you know any man who's ready with a bottle of scotch on hand is all right by me."

Margaret nodded but wondered to herself if Keith on the other hand was "all right" by Robert. She would suspect no.

CHAPTER ELEVEN

BLANCHE

The family had referred to the room across the drawing room as the library. Blanche stood in the center of that room and remembered all of the times, happy times. One wall was filled with built- in bookcases. In the corner fronting the window was Nathaniel's baby grand piano. She ran her hand over the keys, the off key tinkles filling the otherwise silent dwelling with its strange tone. She had never learned to play, despite weekly lessons for some time. Her mind did not work that way.

The piano had been the final piece in Nathaniel Magruder's work of art: the interior of 1304 Thirty-Fifth as he envisioned it. Blanche had been told the story many times....

Nathaniel had his eye on the lot denoted as 1304 on Thirty-Fifth Street for a while. On his walk from the rented rooms in the boarding house to his job, he would often take a detour and cut through Thirty-Fifth to observe the construction. It was considered speculative building and lots were filling up at a rapid pace with dwelling houses.

A cautious man, it took Nathaniel some time to make a

decision of this nature---despite the consistent naggings of his wife, Louise, who had numerous children already hanging from her apron strings in the two room flat that they rented.

One day on one of his jaunts down Thirty-Fifth, he noted a man in high waistcoast puffing on a cigar while overseeing the work.

"Excuse me, my good man," Nathaniel said. "I would like to inquire about this lot here." He pointed to 1304.

"Ach. You donna want that one," the man said with a Scottish accent.

"Why not?"

"That land lay too low there. We filled in."

Nathaniel thought on this and then said, "So I can buy it at a lower price?"

The Scot raised an eyebrow. "You have to build single house there. I lose out." He gave a shrug of his shoulders.

"Single house?" Nathaniel asked.

"Aye. A house on tis own."

Even better thought Nathaniel. A single family dwelling with space on either side. He verbalized his thought. "So...what's wrong with that?"

"Cost me more, it does."

"Well, how can we work this out, sir?"

The man reflected on the stub of his cigar. After some moments he replied, "If we shorten the rear of the house, mabbe it kin be done."

"And the price for me?"

"Will be satisfactory."

The two made plans to formalize the arrangements and shook hands. Nathaniel went home that evening with happy news for his wife.

The Scot made good on his word and the house slowly rose up from the lot with Nathaniel paying close attention whenever he *had the spare moment to do so. On weekends, Nathaniel, Louise and the children (already five by that point) packed a picnic basket and sat in the rear with the half built in the background. Louise would chatter away about all the flowers she envisioned for their private oasis. On one such occasion, not paying attention to their rambunctious boy child, Charles, led to him stepping on a nail and a pell mell to get to medical care for its removal.*

The bottom half of the dwelling was constructed of brick courses running up to the first floor window ledge. A brick chimney rose up from the east side of the house. The remainder of the dwelling was framed out and covered in clapboards. The eight over eight windows were protected by shutters hinged into each side with thick bolts. A tin metal roof filled in the space between gable ends.

Ornamentation was minimal. The Scot had kept the dwelling as basic as possible due to the specs of the contract. That was okay by Nathaniel. His vision lay within the interior of the house where he had great plans.

After the entire street had been filled in with various dwellings, the finished product resulted in very few single family houses like theirs. Most of the dwellings connected to each other as town houses. On either side of 1304 there were stretched rows of three to four townhouses. It set 1304 apart.

But the real surprise that one would never guess was the interior...

After an unexpected windfall of a bonus at work, Papa had announced over a dinner of boiled potatoes and beef that he had purchased a piano. The sisters had looked around at each other with some astonishment since none of them, including Papa, played the piano.

IIe went on to instruct them on where to prepare the

perfect spot in the drawing room for the piano when it arrived by livery service the next day. When the baby grand piano made its way to 1304, the final check was made on Nathaniel's list of acquisitions.

But alas none of the Magruders took to the fine instrument in terms of actually playing it. Their minds did not work in that manner. None were blessed with musical prowess or talent. It was of no bother to Nathaniel. All he had really wanted was the item to complete his vision of the room.

It wasn't until Blackwell Swann made an appearance in the room that the piano was put to the test. Blanche's suitor had been invited over for inspection by Nathaniel. After a dinner of roast chicken and biscuits, the family gathered in the drawing room and Blackwell had moved his fingers lightly over the ivory keys.

Nathaniel had raised his eyebrows and queried, "Do you play, Mr. Swann?"

"Some," Blackwell had answered enigmatically.

"Well then...by all means, please play us some tunes."

Blackwell nodded in acquiescence and began to play a lilting tune from the previous decade of the 1850s.

Blanche smiled widely and perched herself on the front edge of the piano where she could stare at Blackwell. He reminded her of one of the marble statues of Roman men that the Corcoran Gallery of Art held. A broad forehead that spoke of his magnificent intellect, high cheekbones and an aquiline nose was just the start of his visage. Adding to it were his dark eyes and a fine head of jet black hair that he kept on the longish side. Blanche felt that she could never ever tire of staring at him.

The rest of the family settled into the horsehair cushions and sat back to eye up Blackwell for different reasons than Blanche and to listen to his skills. Blanche felt as if her heart would burst with pride and pleasure in Blackwell's impromptu performance. When the piece ended, Blanche and the others clapped merrily.

It wasn't long after that night in the library with her family that Blackwell had asked for her hand in marriage. What a magical night it had been. She had been wearing her blue taffeta gown, the one that everyone said contrasted so vividly with her blonde mane and cornflower blue eyes. Blackwell had been handsome as ever in his military attire.

They had danced at the Officer's Club across the river and midway through the dance he asked the band to play her song, "Fair Bonnie Lass". In front of all the other partygoers, he had bent down on one knee and offered her a marquis cut diamond with emerald chips embedded on each side. She had practically swooned from the happiness of it all.

It was later after his death that someone had mentioned to her that emeralds were bad luck in an engagement ring which could very well explain his demise. She had impulsively thrown the ring down the well in the backyard after hearing it. Later, wishing she hadn't...

Blanche looked around the now darkened room and saw it: the piano in the same place as it had always had been. She sighed heavily. Blackwell...

She shook it off and thought about where in the room would work. Her eyes stared at the wall of books in front of her. The books. She had once been told the true mettle of any book could be put to the test by reading page seventy first. If that page did not strike interest, the book would not be of any interest to a person.

She decided to place a bill in between page seventy and seventy one of books on the wall. Chosen at random. That was it.

CHAPTER TWELVE

Pulling back onto Thirty-Fifth Street, there seemed to be less activity than on other mornings. Margaret thought that maybe they were finally drawing to the end of this exercise.

Mr. Brady, or Robert as they now called him, stood in front of the house with a cigarette in hand. Upon seeing them pull up, he dropped the cigarette and scuffed it out with his shoe. Walking over to the roadster, he put a hand out to assist Margaret.

"Hallo, my good man," said Keith.

Robert tipped his hat towards Keith.

They all made their way into the drawing room. Or what was left of the drawing room.

"As you can see, the couches have been hauled away," Robert said. "We double-checked to make sure all the money was out." He gestured towards some chairs. "We found these old chairs in one of the upstairs rooms. Have a seat."

Three chairs were arranged haphazardly in the middle of the room which now had become more barren with the couches gone. The chairs looked suspicious in their stability, but

Margaret went ahead and edged herself onto the seat. It creaked, but then seemed to bear her weight okay.

Keith sat down and then Robert pulled a chair closer to the both of them and sat himself. His distracted air made Margaret wonder what was going on.

"So...something has come up." He looked straight at Margaret.

She sat still with her hands in her lap. "What is it?"

"First off, I need to ask...did you have a meeting with Lilli Lamb recently?"

Ah, Margaret thought, Lilli Lamb. She answered Robert, "Well, I don't know that I would call it a meeting. She 'invited' me to tea at the White Peacock which was really just a subterfuge to inform me that she had full rights to Blanche's treasure."

"Okay well since that...get together, Miss Lamb has mounted a campaign to usurp you as the guardian and present herself as a better candidate."

"You must be joking," Keith exclaimed. "Margaret is clearly most qualified for the position."

Margaret waved a hand to shush Keith. "Can she really do this?" she asked.

Robert's face scrunched up, and he scratched his head. "Well, she has already had this in the works for a couple of weeks now. She hired a lawyer and he filed the motions a few days ago."

"So...do you mean when I met with her she had already started this up?"

Robert nodded.

"Oh how cheeky," Keith said.

Since their meeting had not gone well...not well at all...Lilli had gone ahead and pulled the final trigger. The wheels were now in motion. But Margaret had been in tight spots before. She could and would take on the likes of Lilli Lamb.

"Will this really proceed into a formal action?" she said.

Robert cleared his throat. "Well, there is some legal precedent here...but I say the best approach is to soothe her ruffled feathers a bit. Maybe get her involved a little in what we are doing?"

"So...we offer a cut of the proceeds, I take it?"

"That...and she also wants a say in where Blanche is housed next."

"Does she offer any ideas or suggestions on that matter?" Margaret asked.

"No...but she wants to have a meeting and go over what places might be options."

Margaret grimaced. In no way did she relish another face to face meeting with Lilli Lamb but in order to preserve her money she guessed she had to.

"So back to her share...what is she expecting exactly?" Keith said.

"After Miss Magruder's needs are met, of course, and all legal fees are taken from the total, she is asking that the remainder be split fifty/fifty between you and her."

Margaret groaned.

"Can she expect that?" Keith said.

"Well, it's a gray area. What would be best is to not let it be tied up in court proceedings."

"Can you think of any way to appease her and give her less than fifty percent?" Margaret asked.

Robert sat back and tented his fingers. "Are there any family heirlooms around that might be of interest to her?"

Margaret and Keith looked at each other. Was there anything at Needham Forest that might work? Old Magruder antiques maybe?

"The problem is I don't know the woman. So I have no idea what motivates her," Margaret said.

"Her lawyer indicated that Miss Lamb seems very nostalgic for family heirlooms. He mentioned something about a teak box?"

She shrugged. "I've never seen a teak box. Were any found here?"

"Not so far. But we still have the well to look into. As you know, the story around the neighborhood was that the big treasure is buried in the well. That is scheduled for tomorrow."

Margaret sat back in the chair forgetting the creaky factor and thought for a moment. Then she said, "How about this? We invite Miss Lamb and her lawyer when the well contents are brought up? Maybe that is where the teak box is...."

"But then we just hand the box over to her? That hardly seems fair, does it?" Keith said.

"It could be a gamble that pays off. What if we offer her whatever is in the well as her pay off. And that only. She signs up for getting only what's in the well."

"Mrs. O'Keefe, I mean Margaret, are you sure you want to take that risk?" Robert asked.

Margaret nodded. "I think by now I have an inkling of how Blanche operated. The well is an obvious place don't you think? There may be something in there but I would bet it is not what all the rumors would have us believe."

"I can have papers drawn up to this effect and see if Miss Lamb and her lawyer are willing. I warn you though, they may not agree to this and we'll have to renegotiate."

"Fair enough," Margaret replied as she stood up and dusted off her pants. "Well, we still have work to do." The men stood up after her.

"I am going to go through those books in the library," she announced to both of them.

"My dear, don't you remember I checked through all of those the other day?" Keith said.

"I know that, Keith, but it came to me while we were driving home the other night. Something about the books...I just want to check again."

Keith shrugged, and Robert said, "By all means, we will certainly indulge any of your ideas on the matter here, Margaret. But we have started boxing them up just so you know."

Keith and Robert trudged upstairs for more work in the bedrooms while Margaret made her way into the library. Like the drawing room, the room had become more barren as the receiving days had progressed. In fact there was nothing on which to take a seat. Some old blankets were stacked in a corner and Margaret dragged one over to kneel on putting thoughts of insects and the like aside. Better that than the hardwood floor pressing on her knees. Boxes sat in disarray in front of her. She also looked up and noted the built in bookshelves still held some books as well.

She sighed and looked around the room. In its heyday, it must have been quite nice. Some wallpaper bits left on the wall still showed a delicate rose pattern that one would be hard put to find these days. She imagined it still filled with the furnishings that had been here and realized that there had been a lot of care placed in making this a nice room. She wondered who had orchestrated that. Her grandparents? Her aunts? She shook her head and felt some remorse that she had not known all of them better. That their lives had not been a part of each other's, more meshed together as a family.

As she opened the first box, dust rose up and she felt the tickle in her nose that she was now accustomed to. After sneezing it out, she began to pull out book by book. She made a careful exercise of letting all the pages fan out. If pages were stuck, she made a point of unsticking them page by page. It almost became meditative after a while.

After about an hour, Margaret had been through two boxes and had accumulated a very tiny pile of things: two four leaf clovers, a few hairpins, several postcards and a newspaper clipping. She sat back with her knees pulled up to her chest and circled her arms around them thinking this could all be for naught.

But she had been meticulous this far so she resolved to continue. In the third box, she found it: between pages seventy and seventy one, there was a hundred dollar bill in a book. Then another book in the same box, again she found a hundred dollar bill, and again between the same pages. She began working at a swifter pace and soon discovered that page seventy was the key.

After the boxes, she stood up and stretched out the kinks. She could just barely reach the books in the bookcase. Dragging them all down made for messier, grimy work but she now knew where the money was and paid no mind to the muss.

By the time Keith and Robert came down to check on her, they found Margaret coated with dust and grime, a big grin on her face. She held out her hands, showing off a collection of bills that tallied up to one thousand dollars.

Later, pacing the center hallway of Needham Forest, Margaret found herself restless. Without putting too much thought in it, she plopped down next to the telephone and picked it up asking again to be connected to the number in New York City.

Judith answered on the first ring.

"It's me, Judith."

"Oh hello, Margaret." An awkward silence occurred before Margaret interjected.

"I thought...well, I thought you might be interested in hearing the latest."

"Go on..."

Margaret explained about the receivership and the monies collected and then she said, "Do you remember Lilli Lamb?"

"Lilli...Lilli...oh yes. The plump little girl who we sometimes saw on occasion. She was quite odd, wasn't she?"

"Yes, that is my memory of her too. And to be blunt she's still odd. And she also has her eye on what she is calling 'the Magruder treasure'."

"Oh surely there can't be that much money left in that old house."

Margaret side-stepped Judith's comment by saying, "Well, she seems to feel she's owed by the sisters. Claims that she visited and took care of them."

Margaret could almost see the contemplative look on Judith's face before she said, "If that was the case, how did the last one end up in the poor house?"

"Exactly. Anyway, I'm working through it with the lawyers."

"Better you than me, old gal. I just couldn't be bothered.... so the auntie is completely blotto then? Bats in the belfry and all that?"

"Well she is.... but she isn't. There seems to be a part of her still there," Margaret replied.

"Hmm."

"But look. I haven't even asked. How is your latest play going?"

Judith perked up. "Oh it's going so well, Mags." She went into a complete description of the performances, costuming and all the rest.

Margaret stifled a yawn and hoped she was expressing

appropriate interest. She wanted to be interested in what Judith was doing. She really did.

Judith wound down and said, "Oh look at the time, doll. I'm running late now for rehearsals."

When Margaret hung the phone up, she felt the nerve bristles of irritation that she always seemed to feel about Judith. She was so self-involved but then Margaret had to ask herself whether the same could be said about her. She shook her head as if to dispel the thoughts. Really, Judith was just enjoying what she enjoyed. Was there anything really wrong with that?

CHAPTER THIRTEEN

BLANCHE

In the back bedroom, Blanche sat in an unlady-like fashion with legs splayed out on either side of her. Bags in front of her had come from the back of the closet. She had run short of ideas, but the bags might provide some.

She pulled one bag closer and opened it. Musty odors drifted up as she dug through it carefully. It was filled with rags, but small ones...the memory came to her quickly. The sisters had all used these to curl their tresses. Mama saved everything and the rags were used over and over again to work their hair into curls.

Maybe they were still useful after all these years. The money and the rags. The money and the rags. She picked one up and stared at it. She then placed a bill from the teak box next to a rag and the inspiration hit. Just as she used to vine a thick strand of hair around the piece of cloth, she began to vine the bill around it. While she wrapped the rags with the bills, she thought about her father and the money....

Emily had finally told Blanche the story of how the money came to be in the house after Virginia died. Before Nathaniel became incapacitated by arthritis, his uncle had summoned him for a visit to a Magruder family farm out in Maryland, Needham Forest. Nathaniel had hired a horse and buggy from the local livery on Wisconsin Avenue and had left for the day, taking Virginia, the eldest daughter with him. Blanche and Emily had been left behind, suspicious but uninformed. They had become accustomed to their father rarely leaving the house.

Virginia had retold the tale to Emily after their father had died and then Emily told the story to Blanche after Virginia died:

The ride out to the countryside had taken a couple of hours as some of the roadways were rutted after a long, hard winter. The trip had not been an easy one. The house had finally become visible on the crest of a hill beyond the turnpike and Virginia had breathed easier. The tree lined drive had some green poking through but it had still been too early in the season for much foliage. The two story brick edifice had a slight abandoned air to it. Perhaps related to being the home of just one soul for so many years.

"Hooahh!" the liveryman called to the horses. He stepped down with a light step to tie the buggy to the hitching post. He reached out to help Nathaniel with his cane and Virginia after Nathaniel.

Nathaniel said to the man, "Go down to the barn for watering and hay. I'm sure he's got some in there. We won't be more than a couple of hours."

Two hours later, Nathaniel and Virginia walked out the front door as promised with Nathaniel struggling to carry a small trunk that donned a small silver padlock. The liveryman eyed it up but said nothing. The trunk was reminiscent of those that immigrants might have carried from the Old World.

Nathaniel yelled over to the driver, "My good man, could you please assist with this end here?" Upon this, he stumbled over the slate walk but righted himself before dropping the trunk. The livery man stepped down and did Nathaniel's bidding.

Between the two men they hoisted the trunk up to the bed of the livery wagon. The exertion was too much for Nathaniel. Virginia turned to him in alarm. "Papa! Your face is so pale."

Nathaniel took out his handkerchief and wiped his brow of the cold sweat that had formed there. "I just need a moment to catch my breath, my dear."

She said, "I worry so about your heart…" The rest was left unsaid.

Once Nathaniel and Virginia were situated back in the buggy, Nathaniel gave a nod and they went back to the city.

Later, at the house, Nathaniel had carefully taken out the items in the trunk. Books and diaries pertaining to family members had been the bulk of the weight in the trunk. The most important item had been wrapped in a small piece of gray wool: a teak box decorated on top with rose quartz pieces. In that box lay the Magruder wealth.

Nathaniel Magruder had been a descendant of a long line of patriots from Maryland who had known great wealth and privilege. Wealth and landholdings, however, petered out over the generations. In families of twelve children (which was the norm), the bounty was divvied up and divvied up again and again over time.

By the time it got down to Nathaniel's generation, it left him a working man putting in an honest day's effort. Some far flung relatives had hung on tighter to the Magruder wealth probably descending from the oldest sons and down. Nathaniel had maintained contact with a bachelor great uncle in that line. Thus, towards the end of his natural born days, Nathaniel's fortunes changed upon inheriting forty thousand dollars from that uncle.

The money fell into Nathaniel's hands yet he didn't really know what to do with it. He had become infirm and he had already procured all the household possessions he had ever wanted or desired. His three unmarried daughters, Virginia, Emily and Blanche, cared for him in the house they had all lived in since the 1840s. He had never had a head for numbers---nor did his daughters. He decided to keep the money in bills in a teak box with a little silver key for the lock. He hid the key in a china teacup that had been a particular favorite of his wife, Louisa, who was now long deceased. And only Virginia knew about it.

He passed on followed in quick order by Virginia. On her deathbed, she told the next oldest sister, Emily, about the fortune in the teak box and the key in the teacup. And lastly Emily showed Blanche the teak box.

So the end of the tale for Blanche was that she was left with no head for figures, a dilapidated house...and a huge fortune. It was her time to make all amends and do what was expected of her. She was trying...one task at a time.

Soon her task for that evening was done. Lying on the floor around her were around thirty rag curls with bills intertwined. She needed to find a place for them now.... an old burlap sack lay on the floor of the closet. She pulled it over to her and began filling it with the thirty pieces.

After standing up, she picked up the bag and headed to the first floor. She grabbed a candle and a matchbox from the sideboard in the hallway and then carefully stepped through the hall to the rear door. Standing on the patio, she breathed in deeply the night air redolent with the smells of spring. Stepping away from the house, she made it out onto the alley, burlap sack in hand, candle and matchbox in her housecoat pocket.

Moonlight gave her enough illumination to see the sewer

grate ahead of her. Once there, she looked around to ensure there was no one watching and then pulled on the grate top. It moved easily enough. She pushed it over to one side. With the burlap sack around her wrist, she squeezed her body through the opening and her slippered feet found a stair step, working their way down. Once down on solid surface, she let her eyes adjust to the darkness, wiping away cob webs that clung to her face and clothes. She reached into the pocket where she had earlier squirreled away the candle and matchbox. Lighting up the candle, she could see the narrow tube-like channels that moved off to her right and left. Pausing, she thought hard about the map.

It was the channel to the right that she needed. With slow and careful steps, she proceeded. The tunnel weaved its way in a curvy fashion underneath the neighborhood of Georgetown and then shifted a little to the left. Blanche stopped at the shift and thought. There was a bench inset into the wall. A couple of feet further there was a ladder stair-up.

This was not her exit. From her recollection, this let out onto M Street. So she burrowed back through the tunnel, the candle flickering and making shadows on the brick laid walls. She felt no fear. Maybe she had become part mole.

She passed by several more exit hatches but knew she was still under Georgetown because of the black Xs on the walls every ten feet. She remembered that about the tunnel.

Blanche had wandered these tunnels so often. Her mind became jumbled and she began to look for Blackwell at every turn of the tunnel, anticipating the light of his candle up ahead

Once underneath the Healy Building ladder stair, she came back to present and realized Blackwell was no more. If only his light had not been extinguished at such a tender age. Sighing, she felt the pain of his loss all over again. She couldn't go any further. She would come back again another time to complete the journey.

She turned and headed back to the X that marked her spot in the tunnel and the exit to her alleyway. On the way she passed the inset bench and, not really thinking much about it, dropped the burden of the burlap sack onto the bench.

CHAPTER FOURTEEN

Again, Margaret found herself at the lawyers' large drawing room-style table, shined to a perfect sheen, reflecting their faces. This time, Lilli and her lawyer sat across from her on the other side of the table. Robert was seated on her side. After an awkward exchange of greetings, the meeting had begun with Mr. Stark at the helm.

He gave a detailed and somewhat mundane account of all that occurred so far with a listing of receivership duties. He then focused on Blanche's upcoming change of residence. Margaret became distracted by his graying handlebar moustache which he frequently fondled with the tips of his right hand fingers as he talked.

"And as I said earlier...the issue of where Miss Magruder goes next is certainly to be agreed upon by all parties..." Mr. Stark continued to pontificate while Margaret let her mind wander off. She wondered if some distant relative would be making the same decision about her fate someday down the road. It wasn't necessarily a pleasant thought...but maybe she needed to think about it.

When Mr. Stark had wound down to a stop, there was a brief silence matched by some awkwardness.

"Well..." Lilli and Margaret both spoke up at the same time. Margaret gave a hand gesture for Lilli to speak first. In a game of strategy she always considered it appropriate to give the opposing party the edge if it in no way impacted the outcome.

"Firstly, I would like to say that I am just appalled by the conditions at Blue Plains. Beyond appalled really." Lilli looked around for support of others in the room. As best Margaret knew, Lilli had never even been to Blue Plains but she said nothing.

Not really seeing any support around the table, Lilli continued. "So I have found a wonderful little place near where I live in Glover Park. I could check in on Aunt Blanche often and I think it would be ideal."

Margaret sat back a bit in her chair and considered what Lilli said. Was it one upsmanship? Did she think Margaret would get jealous by the idea?

"By all means," she said, "if the expenditures allow for it, I have no objections."

Surprise flitted across Lilli's face. "Really?" she said.

"If you are that close to Blanche, of course I think it's wonderful that you could visit so often."

Lilli looked nonplussed as Robert said, "We also have come up with several other recommendations that you may want to peruse...both of you, of course." He pushed forward several pamphlets for the two women to look at.

Margaret looked up from the pamphlets. "Has anyone asked Blanche?" she said.

Robert and Mr. Stark exchanged looks. "Well no. . . we didn't think..." he said.

"Maybe we should though," Margaret said.

"Of course," Lilli piped in. "Of course we should."

"To be honest, ladies.... her communication skills at this point..."

"Well, she has had lucid moments though, right?" Margaret asked.

"That is true," Robert said. "She knew her name and what year it was when Margaret...um...Mrs. O'Keefe and I were there for the competency proceedings."

"For most, one trip to Blue Plains is enough to last a lifetime," Margaret said. She looked pointedly at Lilli and then continued. "But I will go and ask her."

Lilli averted her eyes to one side, making no offer to go with Margaret. Robert spoke up. "I would be happy to escort you back to Blue Plains, Mrs. O'Keefe."

He turned to Lilli. "Would you like to accompany us, Miss Lamb?"

Lilli demurred. "It's not possible for me to take any more time off from my employ. I have already pushed the limits on that with all that I have done."

Margaret sat with a face of stone at Lilli's pronouncement, but remained silent.

"Alright then," Robert said. "I will make the arrangements for another visit, Mrs. O'Keefe."

The meeting broke up and, as all parties dispersed, Margaret caught Lilli staring at her in a befuddled way. Lilli apparently didn't know what to make of Margaret, but Margaret thought she knew exactly what to make of Lilli.

CHAPTER FIFTEEN

BLANCHE

Staring down into the well, Blanche thought she could see a reflection of something. Maybe it was just the moonlight, or maybe it was something else. Maybe it was the glint of the emeralds in her engagement ring. But there was no way to get it back, ever.

She held the teak box under one arm. Though it had been a tedious exercise, she had become attached to the box and would miss it. But the job was done. This was the final step.

She opened the box up one more time. The tattered velvet-lined inside was now empty, bereft of the contents it had held for so many moons. She locked it with the silver key one last time.

Closing her eyes, she stood in front of the well and let the box and the key fall out of her outstretched hands and deep into the well. Hearing a thud but not any sound of its landing deeper.

She had fulfilled the promises and kept the secrets. She had made all amends and done what was expected of her.

CHAPTER SIXTEEN

Word had leaked out that the workers at 1304 Thirty-Fifth Street were moving operations to the outside at the well. Reporters who had been covering the story scurried over for the big break in the ongoing saga. Spectators gathered in the alley and peered over the back fence.

Margaret and Keith were escorted to the rear by Robert upon their arrival. They had not arrived early enough to beat the crowds. They stood on the patio and took in the almost carnival-like atmosphere. "Where are the guys selling soda pop?" Keith whispered to Margaret. She shushed him.

Margaret looked over towards the well and took note that Lilli Lamb and her lawyer stood close by. Robert had pulled her aside earlier to inform her that Lilli had agreed to the deal. She would get all recovery from the well and in return Margaret would get the remainder.

"She's here," Margaret said quietly to Keith.

"Where?" he asked looking around.

"By the well."

Robert gestured for them to move closer. They chose a spot on the other side from Lilli and her counsel.

Robert then spoke to the small group gathered by the well which included several others from his office and a reporter who had been let in along with the workers. "So...in accordance with our proceedings, we will now lower some tools down into the well. And see what we can recover, if anything. Any questions?"

As he looked around the group, Lilli Lamb spoke up in a whiny tone, "I have a question. How do you know this is the proper way to recover what may be down there?"

"Well, Miss Lamb, we've spoken to several noted authorities with expertise in this area and are using their recommendations." He hesitated for a moment and then asked, "Is there something you would like to specify be done here?"

"Well, no. But I want to make sure that all is as it should be."

"Yes, ma'am. We all want to recover whatever is possible. So without further ado. You may proceed, Davey." He directed the last remark to the tall, thin man with a rich skin tone in contrast to his light-colored eyes who appeared to be in charge of the well project.

So it began, the dumping out of years of old soil, leaves and trash. After a bucket came up, it was sifted out on an ad hoc station that was set up close by. It was tedious work and much dirtier than the inside efforts. A horrible earthy stench rose up from the well as the work was conducted.

Soon those gathered all backed up several feet or more to avoid getting splattered on and to escape from the smells. Keith wandered over and perched himself on the edge of the patio, lighting up a cigarette once situated. Margaret joined him. Lilli talked to her lawyer in exaggerated whispers. Margaret could not stand to even look at her. She began to chat with Keith about a horse she had set her sights on at an upcoming auction.

A shout went up over at the well. All hurried over to see what was found. A rectangular sized box caked in a thick coating of earth lay on the sifting table. All watched closely as

Davey carefully scraped off the earth in layers. When he got down to the base coat, he pulled over a bucket of water and used a rag to reveal what was underneath. Little glimmers of pink emerged from under the rag. Lilli let out a squeal. "That's it! The teak box!" She grabbed on her lawyer's arm and tugged with excitement.

Margaret kept a neutral expression while her insides churned. Had she made a drastic error in judgement?

Davey looked up after examining the sides of the box. "It's got a lock on it," he said to Robert.

"Okay, are we all in agreement to have Davey break the lock?"

He looked at Lilli who said, "Yes absolutely!" before shooting a triumphant smile at Margaret. Then he looked at Margaret who nodded.

Placing the box on the flat surface provided by the patio, Davey gently cracked the lock, which required minimal effort after being immersed for so long in the moist underground environment. Davey then stepped back and let Robert step over to the box.

"Ladies and gentlemen, this is it." Taking a deep breath, Robert lifted the lid. It stuck, and Davey came over and ran a putty knife around the edges.

"Try it now, sir."

This time it lifted right up. Every one gathered closer almost heads touching and looked down into the box...into an empty space.

"What?" Lilli exclaimed with a shriek in her voice. "Where's the treasure?" Then she whirled around to Margaret. "You tricked me! You knew all along."

Robert interjected. "It is not possible that Mrs. O'Keefe knew about this. We have documented all proceedings and can show you as such." The last bit he directed to Lilli's lawyer.

The lawyer drew Lilli back a bit and spoke to her in pacifying tones. She visibly fumed the entire time. Margaret snuck a glance at Keith who winked back at her.

"Well recovery will continue as we have not reached bottom yet," Robert said.

As the work continued, Margaret and Keith again positioned themselves on the patio. The sun hid in and out behind the clouds but otherwise the weather was fine for being outside.

"So what is the teak box story?" Keith asked Margaret.

"I really don't know. Or I don't remember ever hearing about it."

"Well, Lilli knows about it. That's for sure. Should we ask her about it?"

"She's not going to give me the time of day, Keith. How about you ask her?"

He groaned.

"Why don't you go over there and manipulate her with that O'Keefe charm? She'll never know what hit her. Besides, we've got nothing else to do while we wait. I'll pretend to read my book." Saying that, she pulled out The Equine Bible from her bag and held it up.

"Okay, okay," he grumbled.

While pretending to become engrossed in her book, Margaret kept an eye on Keith and observed him as he moseyed around the yard pretending to look at plants...or things. As he got closer to Lilli, she looked over at him and sniffed.

As Margaret had suspected, Keith quickly engaged Lilli in a deep conversation. She had a thought that maybe she should be more concerned about what Keith did when he wasn't with her. How many ladies was he off charming or worse on a daily basis? She set the thought aside as she really didn't care to think about it.

In short order, he even had Lilli smiling and then guffawing. But Lilli probably didn't get much male attention, Margaret guessed. So she was almost too easy of a mark for Keith.

Eventually, he made his way back over to Margaret. "Book any good, dear?" he asked with a twinkle in his eye.

She grinned at him. "Yes," she said. "I'll tell you all about it...later."

Another hour passed by before Davey pronounced that there were no further items of value or interest that had been in the well.

Robert handed Lilli the teak box and said something in tones too low for Margaret to hear. Lilli had a mulish look on her face as she stormed off with her lawyer around the side yard.

Robert walked over to Margaret and Keith. "Well, that wraps up recovery in the well. I don't know how you managed it, Margaret, but your gamble really paid off, didn't it?"

She smiled at him. "Lilli is accepting the loss I take it?"

"I hope so. I just informed her that the terms of the agreement we signed off on earlier were met. Even if she doesn't fully understand it hopefully her lawyer will set her straight."

Margaret stood up from the patio ledge and dusted off her pants. "Well...keep us informed then, Robert."

She and Keith walked around the side yard tracing Lilli's footsteps. Back in the Keith's roadster, they headed back to the farm. Once out of city traffic, she turned to him and said, "Well?"

"Do you want the whole conversation or just the highlights?"

"Highlights, please."

"So.... when she finally warmed up enough I asked her about the box. She claimed there was a wonderful tale passed down in the family, told to her by her grandmother. The story goes that Nathaniel travelled very far to receive the box from a relative somewhere and its origins go back to Scotland." He shot a quick glance over her way and added, "Why don't you know this by the way?"

"Scotland?" Margaret asked, ignoring Keith's last question.

"That's what she said. She has romantic notions about the box all tied up with childhood yearnings to know her family better along with the devastation of her parents both dying. I think she's kind of a sad character if you want my opinion."

"Hmm. Don't be fooled, Keith. She's looking for a pay out."

"Well, she won't get it now, will she?"

"Not if I continue to pay attention and stay a couple steps ahead of her..."

<h1 style="text-align:center">CHAPTER SEVENTEEN</h1>

Margaret waited on the steps for Robert to arrive. Keith had offered to come to Blue Plains with her in a halfhearted manner but she preferred to take on Blanche alone---with Robert waiting in the wings should anything untoward occur.

Keith had dropped her off, taking the opportunity to play a game of billiards somewhere in this northeast quadrant of the city. Keith was a man of many secrets. How did he know there was a billiard hall nearby? She hadn't thought to ask him.

Margaret put her face towards the sun, enjoying its warmth. With her eyes closed and up to the sun, she heard rather than saw Robert's town car make its way up the hill and onto the circular drive in front of Blue Plains.

She opened her eyes and watched him nimbly climb out of his automobile with brief in hand. Straightening his tie, his eyes found hers and he smiled. She lifted a hand in a wave from the top of the marble stairs. They were becoming quite a pair, the two of them.

"Nice day out," he said once he reached the top step.

"It is that."

"Shall we?" He put a hand out for her to go ahead. At the

doorway, she rang the gong, which was answered in short order by an attendant.

After signing in and walking down the corridor, they were met by a nurse.

"You are here for Miss Magruder?"

They nodded.

"You're in luck. She's doing real good today."

"How so?" Margaret asked.

"She's chatty and seems to have her wits about her, is all I mean."

"Well that's good then," Robert said.

They were ushered back to Blanche's bed. She was housed with many others in one large room. Curtains hung off windows in various states of disarray so the lighting was dim. Some sunlight streamed in here and there.

Standing at the edge of the bed, Margaret took in Blanche who did indeed seem much different than her last visit to Blue Plains. She was seated upright and brushing her hair with slow gentle strokes. She hummed to herself.

Her cornflower blue eyes focused in on Margaret. "Oh hello. You're back."

Margaret, with some surprise, said, "Do you know who I am?"

"You're one of the nieces. It's Margaret, right?"

Margaret nodded slowly.

"Have a seat," Blanche continued, pointing to a rickety metal chair that sat haphazardly near her bed.

"Thank you...Aunt Blanche."

"To what do I owe the pleasure?" As she spoke, Blanche continued to brush through her hair. She began to twist it into a hairdo at the nape of her neck. A thin blue ribbon, almost teal in color, tattered and soiled, was intertwined through the fingers of one of her hands. Margaret was reminded of a much younger woman. It was as though Blanche had never emerged from a certain period of time.

"Well, I thought I'd see how you were doing," Margaret answered.

"That's sweet of you, dear. I have to admit I'm a little concerned about how I got here. You see, I don't remember any of it. Do you know what happened?"

Margaret looked over at Robert who stood discreetly off to one side of the room but within earshot. He gave an "I don't know what you should say" shrug.

Margaret decided to tell her the truth as she knew it to be. "Apparently, you had some sort of fainting spell on the sidewalk on Thirty-Fifth Street. A neighbor gave the alert and, well, they brought you here."

"Did I hurt my leg?"

"I...I don't know for sure."

"Well it's giving me some pain, I can tell you."

A silence took over in which Blanche starting humming again. Margaret was again struck by the much younger demeanor that Blanche took on.

She stopped humming abruptly and said, "So when can I go home? Are you here to take me home?"

"Oh. Well...there have been a few problems at the house..."

Blanche tilted her head to one side with a practiced coquettish look. Margaret was taken aback for a moment at the mannerism but then continued.

"I don't want to upset you but...there was a break in." She paused to gauge Blanche's reaction.

"Really? Did they damage anything?" Blanche's face twisted itself into a fearful look.

"They found some things."

"Things?"

Margaret took a deep breath and then plunged in. "They found hidden money in the house. In all sorts of places..."

"Oh goodness. How strange!"

"Did...did you know about this?"

Clear and lucid-like blue eyes looked at Margaret. "No, of course not," Blanche said. "Only a silly person would do something like that."

Margaret looked down at her lap, unsure of how to proceed.

When she looked back up, Blanche was again twirling a strand of hair around her finger, seemingly unconcerned about her house. Margaret noted that the teal blue ribbon stayed between her other fingers throughout. She had assumed she would work it in somehow to her hairdo but that never happened.

Taking her eyes off the ribbon, Margaret asked, "So, Aunt Blanche, we were wondering where you would like to go next."

"Go?"

"Yes, we can take you to a nicer place. One with your own room."

"Oh that would be nice. Sometimes it's so loud in here at night." She looked around at the other inhabitants in the beds around her and frowned.

"I can imagine. Lilli Lamb suggested..."

Blanche jerked upright. "Oh no. I'm not going anywhere Lilli goes. That awful girl is out for our money. Emily and I both decided a long time ago that we were not going to be pushed around. She's family and all that but no..."

Margaret put up her hands in a placating manner. "Okay, okay. There's a nice place up off Wisconsin Avenue in Glover Park. Do you like that area?"

"That might suit. Yes, that might suit fine." Blanched nodded after saying it.

"How about I take a look at it and then if it looks okay you can go there?" Margaret said.

"But I might as well just go back to Georgetown, you know. That would be the least trouble really."

"Okay. We can talk about it after you recover...your leg and everything...at the place in Glover Park."

Margaret stood up to leave. She leaned over the bedstead to kiss Blanche on the cheek. Blanche reached out and grabbed her wrist with more strength than Margaret could have guessed at.

"I know you will do the right thing, Margaret Blanche," she said, looking deeply into her eyes.

It unnerved Margaret and she stepped back too quickly, knocking the chair over on its side. The noise of the chair falling started a whole sea of groans and moans from others in the room.

She quickly picked it up and set it right. She had been shocked by Blanche's use of her full name, assuming that any memory of Margaret being named after Blanche had long faded into the recesses of her mind somewhere. But it had come out just like that.

Robert tipped his hat to Blanche and they left, neither one mentioning the fact that Blanche called out Margaret by her full name. But both wondered what it meant.

CHAPTER EIGHTEEN

BLANCHE

Lying in the bed at Blue Plains for she didn't know how long, Blanche's mind raced from one thought to the next, but mostly she wondered why she wasn't in her own house. She shook her head in the hopes that the reason would come up to the front of her mind. She remembered falling and hurting her leg. Had someone come in to help her? Then her thoughts returned to the teak box and its holdings and what her family had expected from her, what she had done and what she had not done.

She had lain around long enough. In the nights, she would lift herself from the bed and experiment with her sore leg. She soon realized that she could walk on it with ease as long as she didn't torque her knee to one side. Often awake in the evenings, she made plans in her head and waited for the opportunity to carry them out.

One early evening, pandemonium struck the corridor and the guard outside Blanche's communal room had been called into service elsewhere to help quell the problems, probably more of the craziness that often kicked up at that hour for some reason. Blanche rose from the bed and snuck out, drifting down the hallway. The others around her paid no attention, lost as they were in their own circumstances.

She had noted well one day that a custodian's closet had an inner door that was actually an exit to the back field. The custodian had accidentally left it open in full view while she was being herded down the hall by a nurse. She had purposely stumbled so that she had a longer time to study the doorways and make sense out of it. Or maybe the custodian assumed there wouldn't be anyone savvy enough to notice the door. But Blanche did. She kept it in a back corner pocket of her brain for safekeeping. The same back corner pocket that let her remember the things she needed to remember.

Once out in the field she waltzed along on light toes loosely encased by her cloth slippers. The sun was almost done, so the darkness was setting in at just the right time. The cloak of darkness would aid her. Her eyes were still eagle sharp and, besides, she knew exactly where she needed to go.

The field was filled with cherry trees. A gust of wind brought with it some left over blossoms floating down, tickling her face as she began her wandering. She floated down the hill of Blue Plains along with the blossoms. Once at the bottom she stopped to get her bearings. Was it right or left? She went with the left side, which turned out to be the correct choice.

Within minutes she found the slightly off-kilter grate, just where her father's maps had indicated. She squatted down and pushed. It moved after a couple of more pushes. Purchasing enough space to squeeze her body through, her slippered feet found a stair step and worked their way down. Once down on solid surface, she let her eyes adjust to the darkness and then reached into her robe pocket where she had earlier squirreled away a candle and a matchbook. It had not been easy, but some of the nurses were more careless than others, and she had seen a stash of candles and lights in an emergency kit drawer.

Lighting up the candle, the illuminated space revealed narrow tube-like channels that veered off to the right and the left. Pausing, she thought hard about the map. It was the right channel she needed. With slow and careful steps, she proceeded.

The tunnel weaved its way in a curvy fashion underneath the Blue Plains area of the city and then shifted a little to the left. Blanche stopped at the shift and thought. A couple of feet further there was a ladder stair up.

This was not her exit. From her recollection, this let out onto Foxhall. So she burrowed back through the tunnel, the candle flickering and making shadows on the brick laid walls. She passed several more exit hatches and then she knew when she was under Georgetown. Black Xs were crossed on the walls every ten feet.

Walking through now, she thought too late to look for the little doorway. Maybe there was a chance to revisit the bunk room where she and Blackwell had spent so many glorious hours together. She would look for it another time.

There was only a short distance to go after the Healy Building. Finally the candlelight revealed a ladder stair on the left side. That was it. The stair to the grate that lay in the back alley of Thirty-Fifth. She shifted the candle to her left hand and held the stair rung with her right.

A couple rungs higher, she had to blow out the candle and stick it in her pocket. Then she used one arm to push as hard as she could on the grate. Muscle memory came back. This had always been the challenge of the tunnels. The exit from them. But, just like other times, the grate creaked and groaned while she moved it this way and that until it freed open.

She scrambled out in an awkward fashion to the alley. Her robe had a fair amount of dirt but there was not much to do about it. Moonlight let her see enough without lighting the candle and she edged herself over to the side of the alley getting to the rear of her childhood home within seconds. She was back.

The back gate gave a louder than usual creak upon Blanche pushing on it. Blanche slipped through the tight space between the gate and the fence line. Once in, she regarded the back of the house. Dark as pitch of course but that did not deter her. She stepped carefully mindful of broken glass and any other articles that might pierce through her thinly clod feet. She stopped halfway and an "Oh" slipped out aloud. One of her mother's rose bushes had stubbornly resisted the change of seasons and several red roses bloomed. The light sweet scent lay in the air and she breathed it in deeply. Her mother had this whole space planted with perennials that bloomed in the spring and into summer. Sadly, she and her sisters had not had the green thumb and the backyard had slowly fallen into disarray. Shaking the memories out of her head, she climbed up to the patio that met the edge of the rear façade.

The screen door hung on by the one hinge left. The back door underneath the screen was slightly ajar. She pushed on it and entered. Stopping on the threshold, she again pulled out the candle and matchbook and lit up the space. The candle illuminated the back hallway where all the careful piles she and Emily had stacked no longer stood perfectly in place like they liked them to be. Strange…She made her way through the hall to the front through the tight corridor.

Out of breath once she got there, she placed the candle down on the old hall table. There was more space than usual to walk about in the front. They had had piles of things that were no longer there. They had needed all these things but now she could not really recall why they had needed them. She took the candle and moved into the drawing room proper. Stopping, she moved the candle around the room. All was not as she had left it.

The call came into Needham Forest early in the morning. Cassie knocked timidly on Margaret's door.

"Come in. What in the world, Cassie? You know it's too early for me to get up…"

"I know that, Miss Margaret, but Mr. Brady's on the telephone. He say it's an emergency."

Grumbling, Margaret made her way up to sitting and Cassie handed her a dressing gown. Running a hand through her hair, she got her bearings and realized ruefully she felt a slight dizziness, the effects of the extra martini she had indulged in the previous evening.

She let out a big deep sigh and headed down to the phone. Seating herself at the telephone chair, she cleared her voice. "Robert?" she said.

"Margaret. Apologies for the rude awakening. We have a problem. Blue Plains contacted me a bit ago."

"What is it?"

"It appears that Blanche has… for lack of a better term…escaped."

"What? How is that possible? The woman is bed-ridden for God's sake!"

"I know. They want us over there as soon as manageable."

After making the arrangements of what time to meet, Margaret placed the phone back on the receiver and closed her eyes briefly. Struggling up, she called out to Cassie.

"Yes, ma'am?"

She rattled off a list of instructions: coffee, plain toast, Keith getting up and all the rest and headed back to her bedroom to get ready for the day.

Shortly afterwards, Margaret found herself once again barreling down the parkway with Keith at the wheel heading to Blue Plains. There was no cheerful conversation this time and she realized at some point that she was clenching her jaw.

"You do have to admire the old gal for busting out of the place," Keith finally said.

Margaret nodded. "Yes, in a way I don't blame her a bit. I just don't understand how she did it."

Robert was waiting for them when they pulled up in front of Blue Plains this time. After exchanging good mornings, their party of three approached the door of Blue Plains.

Before they could reach the bell, the door swung open. Dr. Michaels stood at the entrance.

"Hello, hello. Please come in."

They were all herded into his office. Margaret briefly noted again the elegance of the room and somewhat expensive furnishings in such stark contrast to the rest of Blue Plains.

Seated behind his large desk, the doctor said, "First off, we express sincere apologies that this has happened. We will help in any way possible to find your aunt, Mrs. O'Keefe. Please rest assured about that."

Robert interjected and asked, "What is being done exactly?"

With wide eyes, the doctor said, "Well, truth be told, it's a real mystery. We have no idea how she escaped or where she could have gotten to. Is there anyway somebody might have arranged to pick her up or take her from here?"

All looked at Margaret. She squinted her eyes and then turned to Robert and said, "Do you think Lilli Lamb would do something like this?"

"Blanche did have a relative visit a week or so ago," Dr. Michaels said. "The staff informed me after the visits that the lady was very disgruntled. Very disgruntled indeed. In fact, she even threatened to report to the authorities about Miss Magruder's lodgings." He sniffed after saying the last.

Funny how Lilli had kept that visit a secret and not mentioned it at the recent meeting. Another one of her absurd games in Margaret's estimation although Margaret had to agree that Blue Plains should be reported to somebody. Who knew what "the authorities" would have to say in how the place was run. Clearly this was the doctor's fiefdom...doctors...Margaret personally tried to avoid them at all costs.

"We will certainly check in with Miss Lamb about the situation. But in the meantime can we assume all the grounds and the buildings have been checked and rechecked?" Robert asked.

"Yes of course. There was only one anomaly found."

"What was that?" Margaret asked.

"A sewer grate lid was askew at the bottom of the hill almost to the road. But probably just some neighborhood kids playing around."

"Still, it might be worth it for us to take a look," said Robert.

"By all means, help yourself."

"Also, the local police have been contacted?"

"Yes. They are due to arrive any minute now."

"We'll go down to the grate and then return for the police meeting."

Dr. Michaels nodded.

Margaret and Keith piled into Robert's town car and they made the short drive down to the entrance gate of Blue Plains. As they drove, Robert said, "This may be a red herring but we might as well have a look see ourselves."

They found the grate lid which was still ajar. Their trio stepped around the area looking down at the ground for who knew what, back and forth. To and fro.

Until Margaret stopped in her tracks. Bending down she picked up a teal blue ribbon. Holding it up in her hands for their inspection, she said to Robert, "This is hers. This is Blanche's ribbon."

"Are you sure?" asked Robert.

"Yes, she was fiddling with it the other day when we visited. I noticed it because the shade is an unusual blue. Almost teal."

"And it's the same one?"

"I think so. The color is so unusual."

"Okay. I think the police need to take this further into the tunnels."

Back at Blue Plains, they found Dr. Michaels entertaining the police with cups of coffee served, Margaret noted, on fine bone porcelain. They informed them of their findings at the grate. A policeman took the ribbon from Margaret as evidence. She hesitated handing it over to him and he had to tug on it gently. She felt odd as though she were betraying Blanche.

"I guess there's no reason for us to stick around here," Robert said with some question in his voice.

"That's correct, sir," the officer in charge said. "We'll let you know as soon as we find her."

CHAPTER NINETEEN

The worker came running out of the rear of 1304 Thirty-Fifth Street as though his pants were afire. Jesse whipped his head around. "What in the dickens is wrong with you?" he said.

"I ain't going back in there," the man with eyes big like saucers said. "There's a haunt in there sitting by a pile of books!"

"What are you going on about, man?"

"I'm telling you, she's sitting in there."

"Come on. I'll go in with you."

The man shook his head while Jesse glared at him with a stern look. The man worked under him and knew if he wanted his pay he did as told.

"Come on. I'll go on in first," Jesse repeated.

The other man kept on Jesse's heels closely until they found themselves in the drawing room. The man had not lied. Indeed, there was a small, elderly lady curled up in the corner leafing through the pages of a book. She looked up at their entrance with a curious expression.

Jesse's underling yelled out in terror. "Lady, don't haunt me!

I ain't got nothing to do with all that stealing that went on here. Don't be haunting me, lady."

Jesse threw up an arm for him to hush and said, "Ma'am...is there something I can help you with?"

"Well..." Blanche looked around her. "It's nice my books are here...but where are all my other things?"

"We got nothing to do with all that," the worker interjected excitedly again.

Jesse took him by the arm and pulled him into the hall. "Can't you see this is a flesh and blood lady, fool? Now go down the street and make a call to Mr. Brady. Tell him there's an old lady here in the house, camping on the floor."

The worker didn't need to be told twice and ran out of the room to do as told.

Jesse went back into the room. "What's your name, ma'am?"

"Why, I'm Emily Magruder, don't you know? This is MY house."

"Okay." He held his hands up. "But...how did you get here?"

"I just told you...I live here. How do you think I got here?"

Jesse scratched his head. "Well...can I get you anything?"

"A cup of tea and some biscuits would suit just fine if you can manage it." Blanche went back to leafing through the book.

Jesse mumbled under his breath while leaving the room. "Cup of tea and biscuits. How about that?" This was a fine pickle he was in now. He suspected his best course of action was to stay put by the well until Mr. Brady came by.

Blanche looked through the pages of Gulliver's Travels and felt pleased to be with her books again. But where were all her other things? Those colored men had seemed nice enough but why were they in her house? She wished she could remember the missing pieces.

An hour later, Lilli Lamb strode into the front room purposefully. Blanche was still seated sifting through her books.

"Aunt Blanche!" she exclaimed, dismay in her voice.

"Oh hello dear. Could you please help me up? I fear I might be stuck down here."

With no hesitation, Lilli hoisted Blanche up. Once on her feet, Blanche said, "I'm a bit wobbly too. Could you please bring me a seat?"

Lilli looked around the room, picked through fairly well with little remaining. One chair lay on its side. After righting it, she led Blanche over and she sat.

Lilli pulled over the old piano stool (now missing its partner) for herself.

"Now dear what happened to Papa's baby grand? We always had it right there in the corner. What have you done with it?" Blanche asked.

"Me?" Lilli said placing one hand on her buxom chest. "Not a thing, Aunt Blanche. I don't know where any of it has gone." She lowered her eyes and added, "You might want to talk to Margaret about that."

"Margaret?" asked Blanche in a querulous tone.

"Yes. Margaret O'Keefe."

"Oh yes. She came to visit me at that horrible place. Did you put me in that place?"

"Of course not. I would never."

"Well, how did I get there then?"

"Well..." Lilli started to explain but then thought better of it. "That's neither here nor there, Aunt Blanche. The bigger question really is...how did you leave there to get here?"

Blanche gazed at a spot off to the left and did not answer the question.

"Aunt Blanche?" Lilli prodded.

"Yes, dear?"

"How did you…"

Blanche interrupted her and said, "I heard you the first time," but said nothing further.

There was some commotion in the rear and Margaret, Keith and Robert entered into the front room.

"Oh thank goodness!" Margaret said rushing over to Blanche's side. "Are you alright? Do you need a doctor?"

"Why ever for, dear?"

"Well…did you spend an entire night in here alone?"

"Of course. I have spent almost every night of my entire life in this house. It is my house."

Margaret stopped herself and backtracked. "Of course it is, Aunt Blanche. It's just…such a surprise to find you here."

Blanche shook her head, a wry expression on her face before saying, "Dear…you really are not making a lot sense right now."

Margaret nodded and looked at the others around her, gauging their reactions. She motioned to Keith to stay put and said aloud to Blanche, "We'll be in the back for a moment."

Keith was left behind with Blanche as the others filed out to the kitchen. As Margaret walked down the narrow hall, she could hear Keith saying in a jovial tone, "So how's tricks today?"

Blanche murmured something in response that Margaret could not hear.

Margaret, Lilli and Robert all stood on the back patio and looked at each other, almost as if surprised to be together once again. Lilli said aloud what they were all thinking. "What do we do now?"

"I have no issues with removing her from Blue Plains straight away," Margaret stated outright. "They are clearly negligent in their duties. And, by the way, has anyone figured out how she made it out of Blue Plains all the way to here? It's just short of miraculous that she's not hurt…or worse."

Lilli nodded while Robert looked deep in thought before

responding. "I think a strong argument could be made to remove her directly...without all the usual paperwork required. However, where will she go?"

Lilli piped in. "I found that lovely place in Glover Park. It's a private house where the lady of the house, a French native, cares for several elderly ladies. Nice meals laid out and all the rest."

"Were there any specifications in terms of her health status?"

"Yes...just that she needs to be somewhat mobile and..." Lilli looked around their surroundings "...clearly I think it can be stated she is that!"

"I agree with you on that point," Robert said. "She seems almost agile in fact. But I do have to tell you ladies that she claimed she was Emily Magruder when Jesse asked who she was."

"Oh no," Lilli said.

Margaret threw up a hand. "Who knows? Maybe she just fell back into her old ways? And anyway, the point now is to keep her out of Blue Plains."

Robert nodded. "Do you need to see this place first, Margaret?" he asked.

"No." She gave a nod to Lilli. "I'm sure we can trust Lilli's judgement on this." Lilli gave a satisfied nod in response, animosities set aside for the moment.

"So...shall we take her there now?" Lilli asked.

They again all looked at one another, puzzling over the oddity of the situation.

Robert nodded. "I can take her in my town car. Miss Lamb can accompany us," he said.

Lilli gushed to Robert, "Oh please call me Lilli. We can all be on first name basis after all this, don't you agree?"

Ignoring Lilli's comment, Margaret said, "And Keith and I can follow in our car."

Lilli reached for Robert's arm. "Robert, shall we walk to the coffee shop to telephone the lady of the house first? I have the number on me." Margaret resisted rolling an eye at Lilli's obvious fawning over Robert.

They sorted out that Margaret and Keith would wait with Blanche while Robert and Lilli made the appropriate phone calls.

Margaret and Keith pulled up in the roadster behind Robert's car into a court style street that was referred to as a "place". The neighborhood had the typical look of upper northwest District of Columbia, leafy trees, wide streets, sidewalks, and a general coziness.

Lilli and Robert assisted Blanche out of the car and Margaret and Keith followed behind them. They all stood in front of the residence where Blanche would be living. A stone edifice, one and a half stories tall, with charming dormers lining the half story, it was well maintained. The front door held a cheerful fox door-knocker. Lilli lifted the fox up and knocked twice.

The door opened and a lady of petite height with wide hips stood at the entrance. "Bonjour, Bonjour," she said. "Come in, please."

She stepped back and their small entourage filled the hallway. Blanche looked around at her surroundings with wide eyes. A confusion of introductions was made after the lady announced herself to be Madame Corot, the patroness of the establishment.

Finally, Robert made a point to say, "Blanche, this is

Madame Corot. She will be taking care of you." He made sure that Blanche faced towards Madame Corot.

"Such a pleasure, mademoiselle. I know you will love it here!"

Blanche gave a distracted smile and Margaret said, "Well, shall we help Blanche to her room?"

"Of course, of course. Ladies only maybe?" Madame gave a wink to the men and Margaret and Lilli each took Blanche by an arm as they made their way through the hall into the rear of the house.

The house was decorated in a French country farmhouse style and took Margaret right back to a trip she had made abroad as a very young woman, before she had married. As they passed a windowed wall, she saw blue glass ware placed in the middle of the frame, the sunlight illuminating the blue.

Blanche shuffled along slowly. It was evident that the day was taking its toll on her. When they got to the room that was to be hers, she headed straight towards the bed and they helped her lay down on it.

"So tired..." Blanche murmured.

Madame Corot began to draw the curtains at the windows. Lilli took off Blanche's shoes and Margaret found a throw on a chair and draped it across Blanche.

Then both Lilli and Margaret looked at Madame Corot almost as though seeking direction.

With hands on hips, Madame Corot said to Blanche, "You rest, mademoiselle, and I will check on you, eh?"

On the bed, Blanche with eyes half closed, gave a slight nod.

Back in the foyer, Keith and Robert stood awkwardly waiting for their return. Robert had his hat in hand and was twisting it around.

Margaret saw the question on both of their faces as she walked forward. "It's fine," she said. "She'll be fine here."

Madame Corot addressed their group and said, "Please do not worry. She will be well taken care of."

They made their goodbyes and headed out the door.

At the cars, Robert said, "We'll be in touch soon." Margaret nodded. Then he looked at Lilli and said, "Where can I take you, Miss Lamb?"

"Remember, it's Lilli," Lilli said with a coy smile. "And it would be so kind of you to take me to my house. I would be ever so appreciative---Robert." She drew one hand up to her hair and fluffed it up as Robert opened the door for her to get in.

Margaret made an inelegant snorting noise as she got into Keith's roadster.

Keith looked over at her. "What is that for?" he asked.

"Did you see how Lilli flirted with Robert?"

Keith shook his head. "I didn't notice...no."

"The gall of her. Clearly, she didn't like that I was on first name basis with him. So once again she's making her point. But thinking that Robert would ever punch her dance card. A woman like Lilli would in no way appeal to a man like him."

"Really? How do you know Robert's taste, my dear?"

"Well, I mean...just look at her. She's not his type at all."

"Hmm." Keith didn't say anymore and Margaret stewed in her own thoughts wondering a bit why Lilli's behavior irked her so.

Later that night, Margaret and Keith relaxed at Needham Forest in the drawing room after enjoying a meal of Cassie's famous pot roast and potatoes. Margaret stretched across the pink Victorian sofa, not too unlike the horsehair sofas at 1304 Thirty-Fifth, and Keith began to massage her feet with his capable hands.

As he rubbed her feet, she said, "It's such a puzzle, isn't it?"

"What's that, dear?"

"Well, the whole thing really. The money. The hiding places. But especially how did she orchestrate the escape from Blue Plains? How did an eighty some year old, incapacitated woman not right in the head orchestrate an escape that took her from one side of the city to another? And she ends up perfectly fine without a scratch?"

Keith chuckled. "That really is a testament to the ingenuity and cleverness of your gene pool, isn't it darling?"

"Hmm. Maybe. If it was the tunnels, how in God's name was she able to navigate through them? I mean just imagine it: the fetid water, the smells, the rats..." Margaret shuddered.

Keith just shook his head and lifted up his martini for a sip.

"Well, the good news is she seems well and fine at her new situation," Margaret said.

"Yes, indeed. Who wouldn't want a meticulous French woman as a caretaker?"

"Are you being sarcastic, Keith?"

"Not at'll. Did you see the place settings in the dining room? That was Quimper from Brittany if I'm not mistaken. A wonderful place..."

"It certainly did seem an opportune set up," Margaret said.

"So really you should be toasting Lilli Lamb for finding it," Keith said.

Margaret grimaced but then said, "I guess you're right." She lifted up her glass to Keith and they clinked.

"To Lilli Lamb," Keith said.

"Who knows?" Margaret added. "Maybe Lilli can figure out how the hell Blanche pulled this caper off."

"Yes...give the devil his due and all that..." Keith said. He let the thought drift off as they sipped their drinks.

Before retiring that evening, Margaret sat down next to the phone and again had the operator connect her to New York City.

When Judith answered, she let out a yawn on the line and said, "Oh it's you, Margaret. I just got in and am just beat."

"How did it go tonight?"

Margaret could almost feel the surprise coming from Judith at her interest in the show. "Well, it went just fine...thank you for asking."

"I know you're tired but I just have to tell you this..." Margaret regaled Judith with the tale of Blanche's escape and the suspicion that she utilized the tunnels under Georgetown to do so.

"My word...that is really something."

Margaret chuckled. "It really is," she said. "I have to say, Blanche reminds me of you. She's got some moxie."

"Why, Mags, I take that as a compliment. I never knew you thought that of me."

"Of course I do. It's not just any woman who can pick up and establish herself as a bonafide New Yorker like you have done."

Judith was oddly without words for a moment but quickly recovered herself saying, "Well, of course, I see some of this moxie in you as well."

"Let's not get too complimentary. Our heads will swell," Margaret replied and then both sisters burst out with a laugh.

"So I have to ask," Judith said. "Do you think all her hiding places are the work of a fool...or the work of a genius?"

"Judith, I have asked myself this question again and again. It's all part of the mystery really."

They ended the call with Margaret promising she would continue to keep Judith apprised of developments.

CHAPTER TWENTY

Blanche studied the tea cup in front of her. The design was unusual - a small girl with a funny hat on. The lady of the house poured the tea into the cup.

"So, ma cherie, you like your eggs scrambled?"

Blanche, with some surprise, said, "Why yes. That would be fine." It had been some time since anyone asked her how she liked her eggs. Some time indeed.

She took a closer look at the lady in front of her who beamed back with good cheer. Her hair was caught in the back but many wisps had fallen forward. A mix of black and white... salt and pepper Blanche guessed it was called. Her eyes were crinkled at the corners indicating good humor on her part. Her skin was ruddy in color.

"I'm sorry. I've forgotten your name."

"Pas de problem. I am Madame Corot."

"And where am I exactly?"

"Aahh. Oui. This is Glover Park. Over there," she gestured with her free hand "is Wisconsin Avenue. You know Wisconsin Avenue?"

"Oh yes. My house in Georgetown is kitty corner to Wisconsin."

"Very well then."

There were empty seats around Blanche with place settings in front of them. "Where are the others?"

"They finished. You were asleep a long time."

Blanche nodded.

Madame Corot left the dining space leaving the café doors into the kitchen swinging to and fro. Blanche looked about the room. A cheery place with lots of light. Very homey. Still.... she would rather be back at her own house. It smelled a little too spicy for her taste. But she wouldn't complain about it. The woman was being awfully nice and accommodating.

The woman soon returned and said, "Voila!" placing a plate in front of Blanche and then sat across from her.

As Blanche picked at the food, the woman began talking. "So you must tell me, mademoiselle, of your travels."

"Travels?" Blanche asked with some confusion in her voice.

"Yes...they told me you went from Blue Plains to Georgetown in the night. How did you do it?"

Blanche chewed a small bite of the eggs as she pondered the question. There was no real point in keeping it a secret, was there?

Looking up from her food, she said, "The tunnels."

"Where are these tunnels?"

"They run all over the place...under the city."

"Vraiment? Really? I did not know..."

Blanche continued, "Yes, my father had the maps years ago. He worked for the city you know. So I learned where all the tunnels are."

"So...there is a tunnel from Blue Plains to Georgetown?"

"Not directly, dear. You have to know what turns to take."

"How did you remember the turns?"

Blanche shrugged. "I just did. That's the thing about getting old it seems. Some things you remember and some you don't. It can be frustrating."

Madame Corot nodded. Then she asked if the eggs were okay.

"Oh yes. Just wonderful." She leaned forward in a confidential manner. "I don't like to complain but the food at Blue Plains..." She made a grimace.

"Well, I think you will like it better here."

"I already do, dear. I already do."

As Madame Corot busied herself cleaning up the breakfast items, Blanche looked around and took in her very pleasing surroundings. Especially without Lilli Lamb around. The bossiness of Lilli reminded her of another time in her life....

On Saturday mornings, their mother, Louisa, handed three cent coins to Emily and three cent coins to Blanche. But really Emily, age twelve, was in charge of all six coins. When the girls began their walk there, Blanche practically hopped with excitement next to Emily. She wore a bright blue smock over white pantaloons in contrast to Emily's drab beige waistcoast. Now that Emily was getting older their mother had changed out her wardrobe to the more austere of the two.

Emily looked over at Blanche noting how the blue of the smock made Blanche's eyes look more blue. She said, "Blanche, give me your coins so you don't drop them."

"No! I won't drop them."

"I said give them over," Emily's voice was tinged with her authority as the older sister in charge.

Blanche stomped a foot and said, "I don't want to!"

Emily's eyes narrowed and she came to a stop. "Fine. I don't have to walk you to Mr. Victor's."

Blanche let out a harrumph and then said, "Alright, alright."

Her fist, still chubby with childhood, unfurled and there laid the coins stuck together. She picked them up one by one and handed them over to Emily who placed them in her little drawstring silk pouch.

"There. Now that wasn't so hard, was it?" Emily said, pleased as usual when Blanche had to give in to her. Blanche thought to herself as she often did, "Bossy, so bossy."

The girls continued on the walk two blocks to the west and one block south until they stood in front of Mr. Victor's Confectionary Shop. Blanche set any anger aside and began to jabber with excitement about the candy she would pick: a peppermint that would dissolve on her tongue with a tingle, a horehound drop with a hint of sarsaparilla and a vanilla cream oozing with flavor.

"What about you, Ems?"

Emily had been walking along with a slight frown. "Huh? Oh, I don't know. Maybe a piece of licorice."

Blanche could tell Emily was in another one of her moods. They walked the remainder of the way without any discourse, with the exception of Blanche humming to a tune in her head.

Soon they stood in front of the plain brick exterior of Mr. Victor's Confectionary which in no way spoke of the riches that lay within. Blanche could almost taste the sugar on her tongue before even entering the shop. When they opened the door, the aroma of sugar tinged air hit them before the bell even jangled.

The center of the room was filled with other children out on the same Saturday morning mission. On either side of the store, long glassed in display cases ran from one end of the store to the other, showing off all different kinds of sweets.

Blanche jostled her way around the other children, gaining purchase at some of the glass space and impatiently waiting her turn. Emily made her way behind her.

Blanche stared at the array in front of her, all the different colors swirling into one. Finally, Mr. Victor pointed to her and said in his German-accented loud voice, "Your turn, Miss Blanche! What is your pleasure today?"

Blanche pointed to her three choices and then turned to Emily for her cent coins. Emily dug them out of the silk pouch and said, "I'll pay him."

"But I want to do it, Emily!"

"I said I will do it."

Blanche felt a rush of frustration towards Emily and wondered why, why she was so bossy.

Mr. Victor handed the small brown paper bag across the counter to Blanche and gave her a wink.

"I put in an extra blue sweet to go with your pretty eyes."

Blanche bestowed him with a big grin and felt Emily bristle next to her.

Mr. Victor looked over to Emily and took her order.

Back out on the street, Blanche dug into her paper bag and tried her blue sweet first.

"Oh this special candy Mr. Victor gave me is so so good. Did he give you something special?" she asked slyly.

Emily's face darkened and she said, "You know very well he did not, Blanche. It's because you batted your baby blues at him. I saw you."

Blanche gave a trill of laughter. "Oh fiddle faddle. You're just jealous, Emily. That's what you are."

Emily said nothing but quickened her pace so she was several strides ahead of Blanche for the rest of the walk.

Margaret was in her den studying some paperwork. As usual, the numbers were not adding up. It had become an exercise in frustration of late. And because of all the activity with Aunt

Blanche she had let it pile up which was not working in her favor. A light knock on the door interrupted her thoughts. "Yes," she said.

Cassie's broad face popped around the doorway. "It's just me, missus. There's somebody on the telephone that says he has to talk to you right now."

"Who is it, Cassie?"

"He won't say, ma'am. I tried my darnedest…"

"Alright." Margaret sighed and stood up.

Once in the hall, she placed the phone to her ear and said hello.

The creditor immediately went into a long-winded exposition on her credit rating and all the rest and fell just short of threatening to take her first-born child (if she had had a first-born child). She felt the tension ooze lava like through her body and her heart rate accelerate. He continued to badger her until she finally interrupted and said she was hanging up as his voice had taken on a particularly surly tone.

An unpleasant individual at best but a precursor to things getting worse. All that betting at the track that Keith had done… she knew something had to shift. She needed access to Blanche's money and she needed it straight away.

She sat on the gossip bench and thought. Then she picked up the line and dialed out.

When Robert got on the line, she dispensed with the niceties and got to the point of the call. "When can we expect that everything will be settled?"

"Well, the tally is in and we just need the final approvals from our accounting department."

"So are we talking a couple of days…or longer?" Margaret asked.

Robert cleared his throat and then said, "Well, we do have one fly in the ointment that needs to be figured out."

"What's that?" Margaret asked, feeling the anxiety rise up a little higher into her chest.

"As you might remember, Blanche had assumed Emily's identity for a while. So that has presented some legal ramifications."

Margaret tamped down the anxiety she was feeling and said, "So what needs to happen?"

"Blanche needs to go in front of the judge and explain."

Margaret let out a groan and said, "But I thought she didn't meet competency levels."

With apology in his voice, Robert said, "I know. But there is some sort of loophole involving her presence in the court room."

"When will that happen?' Margaret said tersely.

"I really couldn't say at this point, Margaret." After some silence, he added, "Is there some sort of problem?"

Taken aback, Margaret tried to cover up. "No, no. Just realizing that I have some travel coming up and would like to have this all resolved."

"Ahh. I see. Well no worries. You can be assured that all will be attended to during any absence on your part."

"Of course, Robert. Your firm has done a fine job."

"Thank you, Margaret. And may I say, it has been a pleasure getting to know you."

"And likewise..." Margaret said, flustered.

Margaret stood up and headed down to the barn thinking of what Robert had said. She needed the distraction of the barn, the only place she could find some peace. She let out a low whistle for Oliver who came scurrying to her side from the kitchen. Oliver generally stayed in the kitchen since Cassie tossed scraps his way throughout the day. Margaret had admonished Cassie that Oliver was getting fat off the scraps to which Cassie had replied, "That won't hurt him none, ma'am."

Margaret had backed off knowing when to choose her battles with Cassie.

"Come on boy. Let's take a walk," Margaret said to Oliver as she grabbed a light jacket off the hook. The act of getting out of the house was already helping lighten her mood.

Once at the barn, Margaret found Leonard leaning over the fencepost watching the horses grazing beyond in the paddocked fields.

"Hello, Leonard," Margaret said.

He looked up and nodded. Then he dug into his jeans pocket and fished out a dog treat absentmindedly handing it to Oliver in his palm. Oliver wriggled his body in appreciation.

Margaret and Leonard were silent as they watched the horses, a comfortable silence common to those who have spent many years in and around each other's company. Then Margaret broke the spell.

She said, still gazing out into the fields, "We're in trouble, Leonard. I can't cook the books anymore to work."

He didn't respond to that but instead said, "I knew your daddy as well as anybody probably. He taught me when I was just starting out. Gave me a chance when no one else would. He would be mighty proud of you, ma'am."

Margaret just shook her head in response.

Leonard continued, "You've just had some setbacks that's all. It's typical enough in this business. That's been my experience anyhow."

After some more silence, Margaret turned to look at Leonard, taking in his weather beaten profile, and said, "Leonard, I think we are going to have to let a couple of the trainers go. I hate to do it. I'll leave it up to you who goes first. You know best the ones that pull their weight more, and the ones that won't grumble too much about the extra work they will have to put in."

Leonard turned and looked at her without much surprise in his expression. A man used to life's tough breaks who didn't react to them anymore.

Margaret continued. "But I don't want you to worry about your job here. It will never be in jeopardy as long as I have a say in it. And I do have a biggest say in it. I am close to getting everything right back on track. Right where it needs to be. I can't say too much more right now. But please know that I am working as hard as I can to make all of this right."

Leonard nodded slowly and Margaret could tell he had something to say. She waited him out and then he came out with it. "Ma'am...I got a buddy who's at the track a lot."

"Yes?" Margaret said. And she had a sinking feeling of what was next.

"Well, he's seen Mr. O'Keefe down there. A lot. I don't like to talk out of school like this and you know that I'm looking out for your own good."

Margaret put a hand up. "Please, Leonard. There is no need to spare my feelings here. Tell it to me straight."

"Alright. He says Mr. O'Keefe is pretty out of hand with the betting and what not. The drink too I guess he means. And there are some fellas there, well let's just say you don't want to get on the wrong side of them, if you know what I mean."

Margaret placed her hands on top of the fence rail staring down at her wedding ring. Then she looked at up at Leonard and said, "Yes, Leonard. I know what you mean. And thank you. Thank you for all you do."

After Leonard left, Margaret strode into the barn and grabbed a pitchfork. She began mucking out Prince's stall, one of her favorites. An American Quarter horse with an unusual dapple gray coat who still cavorted in the fields as Margaret worked. It was smelly, laborious and hot but the physical work took her mind off all the rest. She felt the release of the tension knots in her back.

She heard Keith's voice before she saw him. He said, "Darling, why do we pay all the groomsmen if you are just going to do that yourself?"

"Every bit helps, don't you think Keith?" she said not looking up from the shovelful below.

"Well, that would be true if we paid them by the hour but we don't, do we?"

She tossed the shovel aside and placed both hands on her hips. "Do you really understand at all how much it costs to run this operation?"

He answered her, "Of course I do. We are in this together, darling. We make a pretty good team too."

Keith stood outside the stall, impeccably dressed in his business blues not a hair out of place. Somehow that annoyed Margaret more than any of it. She had the sudden impulse to load a shovel filled with manure on him. But she didn't. Instead she replied, "Do we, Keith? What if one on the team is overspending the profits? Does that make for a pretty good team?

"What is all this about, Margaret?"

She picked the shovel back up and began anew. And said, "Nothing. It's about nothing." Silently she told herself she would handle it. And after she handled it, she would make sure Keith had less access to cash. It wasn't really his fault. He was attracted to things that were bright and shiny. It was just the way he was wired.

Hesitant to say much more, he tried one more time with a plaintive tone in his voice. "Join me for a martini?"

She stopped again to push a wisp of hair out of her face. Without looking at him, she answered. "In a bit. I'll be up in a bit."

CHAPTER TWENTY-ONE

Margaret sat in the sunroom of Needham Forest with breakfast in front of her. Cassie had prepared a poached egg with rye toast points. Some of Cassie's countywide famous homemade blueberry jam had been set into a china cup for Margaret to smear on the toast as she liked. The poached egg sat in a cup designed for that purpose. *Everything had a purpose*, Margaret thought to herself. She picked around at the food with not much appetite eventually setting her fork aside and gazing out the window at the view in front of her: the paddocked fields where the horses had the freedom to run about as they were on this morning.

The trainers must have finished with their morning exercises and the horses were allowed to escape into the early fall morning enjoying all that came with it. Late summer had been slowly releasing into fall. The heavy fugue of humidity that the region was known for in the summer months had begun to lift and cooler airs were in play to take over with the next season. Indeed a glorious morning it was. The sun vibrant in the sky, the trees all in color, grasses and leaves blowing around in the breeze. The horses expressed their delight by nudging each other, whinnying, and being otherwise playful.

Cassie cleared her throat.

Margaret looked up. "Oh Cassie," she said. "How long have you been standing there?"

"I didn't want to interrupt your breakfast none." Cassie stared down at the mostly uneaten food in front of Margaret.

"It's not that it's not good, Cassie. It is of course. I just...I was..."

"You was daydreamin' ma'am. I seen you."

Margaret couldn't help but smile. "You caught me," she said. "I was watching how much fun the horses are having this morning."

Cassie's gaze followed Margaret's to the outside. After staring at the horses for a minute, she said, "Well, anyways, I hate to interrupt but Robert wants you to call him when you can. It's not an emergency he says but just when you can."

"Thank you, Cassie. And you can clear this up...I'm finished."

"You need to eat more Miss Margaret...you're going to waste away you not careful."

"I'll be fine, Cassie. Don't you worry about me."

Cassie walked out of the room with the dishes shaking her head and muttering to herself.

Margaret stood and stretched the kinks out of her back. Making her way into the hall, she sat by the phone and dialed out to Robert's office.

Once on the line, he answered in his now familiar voice, "Good morning, Margaret."

"Robert. How are you this morning?"

"Well, very well. So I wanted to let you know the court date has been set for Blanche to appear before the judge to verify her identity." He went on to give her the particulars.

"Alright then. I will be there. How is Blanche getting there?"

"Lilli Lamb has offered to bring her...she claims that she lives the closest so..." He let the last part hang in air, waiting to see if there would be dissent on Margaret's part.

Margaret was becoming somewhat anesthetized to Lilli and her ways so all she said was, "Let her." It didn't really matter and Margaret was too distracted with her financial paperwork to worry about whether Lilli Lamb was winning more points or not. They wrapped up the conversation and agreed to meet at the courthouse the following week.

Margaret and Lilli sat in the row directly behind Blanche in the courtroom. Margaret took in Lilli's patent leather purse placed neatly on her lap with its oversized metal clasp. It was an ugly clutch and accented her outfit in no positive way. Here they sat, side by side, the strangest of adversaries.

Robert sat next to Blanche. After the preliminaries, she was helped up to the stand and placed into the seat by the bailiff. Then sworn in. As she faced out towards Margaret and the others, Margaret again marveled at the wonder of her aunt. Her father's sister. Here she was sitting with a straight spine in front of the judge and listening with attentiveness.

Madame Corot must have had a hand in dressing her for the occasion. Her dress was clean and tidy and fully buttoned. Her hair had been freshly brushed back into a chignon at the nape of her neck. Her eyes were lively and she was fully alert. Vestiges of the beauty Blanche had been shone through. All in all the move to Madame Corot's had shaved years off of her life.

The judge nodded in the direction of Robert and he began with the prescribed line of questioning. After establishing her full name, age and city of her birth, he began probing with some deeper questions.

"So, Miss Magruder, what year exactly were you born in?"

Without missing a beat, Blanche answered. "1846."

"And your sister, Emily, what year was she born?"

Blanche flickered her eyes around the room and hesitated. Then she came out with the year of Emily's birth. 1840.

"Miss Magruder, how many years did you live with your sister, Emily?"

Blanche looked at him with surprise. "Well, all my life, young man. Emily and I always lived together until...until..."

Robert prompted the end of her sentence. "Until what, Miss Magruder?"

"Until she died." Blanche looked downwards toward her lap.

"How did Emily die, Miss Magruder?" Robert asked.

"How did Emily die?" Blanche looked up and parroted the question back to Robert.

"Ah...yes." Looking down at his notes, he repeated. "How did Emily die?"

The courtroom faded out and Blanche's mind ventured back to that day. It had all been a terrible mistake. That was it. A terrible mistake. Emily had not been feeling well. She had been querulous and demanding too, ordering Blanche about. "Get me a cold cloth for my face." "My tea is too cold. Make me another." All the demands.

Blanche had complied of course. She had always done Emily's bidding. Scales had been tipped to Emily's side for quite some time. In part due to Emily being the older sister. But mainly it was the debt Blanche owed Emily.

How Emily had helped her during the terrible time...but it didn't bear thinking about that.

As that day wore on, the house had become hot. The cool, night air that they let in during the evenings had been sucked up by the humid heat once again. What remained was a fug.... a sultry miasma. As the air thickened with humidity so did Emily's voice thicken with the orders and the demands.

They had been in the library. Emily had started to lecture her, bringing up past grievances in that tone. "You really shouldn't have spoken to the ragman like that, Blanche. You were quite curt with him."

Blanche said nothing in reply.

"Are you listening, Blanche?"

Blanche got up from the chair. "I'm listening, Emily. I've been listening to you for seventy-five years and I'm sick of listening."

Emily gasped and reeled back into the sofa cushions.

Silence filled the space between the two sisters.

Then Emily spoke. "Of all the nerve. Everything I have done for you."

"Everything you won't let me forget for a second," Blanche hissed back without missing a beat.

Emily's faded blue eyes narrowed and she said, "If anyone knew what you had done."

"What, Emily? If anyone knew, then what? Wasn't it always more about you saving face than what I wanted?"

"We did it for the family...you know that!" Emily said her tone now shrill and high-pitched.

"What about me? What about what I wanted?" Blanche cried out.

"Oh you spoiled girl. Always so spoiled. Mother and Daddy giving into your whims every time. On and on about your blonde hair." Emily's face showed disgust all over it.

She then lifted herself up and stood, unsteady in her stance. Her visage was pale and sweaty.

She pointed a shaky finger at Blanche and said, "You are ungrateful is what you are!" And then she began to speak the unspeakable.

Before she could get any more words out and without conscious thought, Blanche struck out with her arm connecting with the tender bones on Emily's face.

Emily fell with her head making a dull thud noise as it hit the hardwood floor planks. Then there was no noise. No shrill tone. No querulous badgering. No hectoring.

Blanche stood still, stuck in place. Emily silent on the floor beneath her. Shaking her head as if to clear the sight from her brain, Blanche then floated down next to Emily.

"Emily," she said shaking her shoulder. "Ems...oh no, no, no, no, no, no..."

Emily's eyes were wide open and a thin trickle of blood had started to make its way down out of one corner of her mouth.

"It was an accident. I never meant to...you'll be fine. I'll get help..."

Blanche flung herself out of the house and down the street.

Later, when the officials came back, she became Emily. She had to become Emily to make it all right again.

The voice repeated the question. "How did your sister die?" Blanche looked around the courtroom at the sea of faces, honing in on Margaret's face, then Lilli's. Did they know? Did everyone know what she had done? How much should she tell them?

The judge cleared his throat and said in a kind voice, "Miss Magruder, we know it's painful but please answer this question."

Blanche's voice came out gravelly. "My sister died of a

stroke. She had a stroke and fell over, hitting her head. They told me it was the stroke that killed her. Not hitting her head."

She looked at the judge and said plaintively, "They wouldn't lie about that, would they?"

"No, no. Of course not, Miss Magruder. Proceed, counselor."

"So at what point did you decide you were Emily?" Robert asked.

"When they came to the door...they asked who I was and I said Emily. Because it should have been me that died, don't you see?"

"Uh...why was that, Miss Magruder?"

"Because.... I was such a bad girl."

People in the courtroom exchanged uneasy glances. Robert himself looked perturbed.

"Well, I'm sure that's not true. Do you think you were confused after the shock of your sister's death?"

"No," Blanche replied without hesitation. "I wasn't confused. I knew what I had to do to make it right."

"Make it right?" Robert echoed.

After some silence, she said, "Everything I had done wrong!"

"What did you...?" Robert said.

Margaret stood up and interrupted. "I think my aunt is under some duress here. Does this questioning need to continue? It is obviously upsetting her."

Robert looked to the judge for guidance. Margaret sat back down and tried to grasp Blanche's thought processes. Was this going to prevent the account from being settled? She didn't know what else to do but interject when she had. Lilli Lamb shifted nervously next to her.

The judge looked thoughtful. "We shall proceed," he said.

Robert began again. "So you were making up for the past wrongs by taking Emily's identity?"

"Yes, you see she was the good one. The good daughter. I tried to live up to her example. I really did. But..." Blanche's eyes drifted off to a corner of the room. "I failed."

"But how would taking her identity fix this?" Robert asked in a gentle voice.

"Why...if I was her, I could be good. Don't you see?"

He cleared his throat before saying, "But you do realize that you are Blanche Magruder?"

She nodded and said, "Of course I realize that."

"Let it be stated for the record that Blanche Magruder assumed Emily Magruder's identity for the purpose of 'righting a wrong' which was only an objective in her mind alone. No nefarious purposes were intended by this identity swap."

The judge was quick to take up the point and stated unequivocally, "The court hereby decrees that Blanche Magruder knowingly assumed her sister's identity but understands that she is the one and only Blanche Marie Magruder." He banged his gavel once causing Blanche's head to jerk.

Lilli and Margaret rushed to the front of the courtroom to assist Blanche out of the box. Blanche had a shattered expression on her face and turned to them saying, "Is everything all right now?"

"Yes, of course, Aunt Blanche. You did fine," Margaret said, comforting her as best she knew how.

"But I didn't tell the whole truth of it."

Margaret looked around before saying, "We'll talk later if you like. Let's get you back to Madame Corot's." They hustled her out of the room.

That afternoon, Margaret sat in front of Robert's desk in his office and studied the spreadsheet in front of her. The numbers were startling even though she herself had pulled money out of tins, paintings, books and horsehair stuffed cushions. She never thought though that it would add up to this amount.

The grand total was $37,451.00. Near to the amount rumored to be hidden in the house. The amount that Nathaniel Magruder had supposedly received from his rich uncle. It came full circle because the house that Margaret now lived in was that same said uncle's house. So her line had not only received the treasure but also the house.

It all was coming down to her specifically. Lilli had made her rash gamble thus depriving herself of any of it. Needham Forest and its horse business were in jeopardy of course but Margaret hoped to finagle the money to get everything back. She had to keep Keith on a tight rein in the meantime.

She thought to the earlier conversation she had with him. He had been at the club and they had not let him put a round of drinks on his tab.

"Quite embarrassing, lovey."

She had replied, "Well that's just it Keith. It is getting embarrassing. Especially if we lose all of it."

He scoffed. "That would never happen."

"We are more than overextended Keith. There is a lien on Needham Forest. And I...we are in grave danger of losing it. I just can't have that. It would be a disrespectful to everything Daddy accomplished in his life and all his hard work."

She fleetingly remembered the sniff of cigar smoke wafting through the barn. Had her father been trying to tell her something?

Keith blustered and blabbered on almost to the point of begging her for a bank draft. Claiming he had a scheduled meeting at the track and had to save face. Promising it would be the last time. It came to Margaret that she had been like an indulgent parent with Keith over the years. No meaning yes every time. Keith knowing he could break her down with his charming ways.

And just like an overindulged child Keith had tantrumed and it had been ugly until she cracked eventually as he knew she would. She put the thought out of her head. Too unpleasant.

This was the day it stopped. She had been handed a way out on a silver platter and she refused to squander it. The cigar smoke reminded her of all that was at stake.

She looked up at Robert and asked, "So...am I able to draw upon the account now...for Blanche's expenditures?"

"Oh, of course. I have it all set up for you. Here are the forms for bank drafts to take out funds as necessary. In the meantime, here at Stark, Wilson and Obermann, we would be happy to invest the bulk in some attractive interest bearing investments that are at our disposal."

Margaret waved a hand. "Oh, no need. I am quite proficient myself with stocks and bonds."

"Oh?" Robert looked at her through his oval shaped glasses.

"Yes. Through my horse operation I am privy to many other business opportunities so I can ensure the funds get put into the most excellent channels with good returns."

Robert's mouth formed a wry grin but his disappointment was evident.

"Well then," he said. "I guess this is it. Let's send you on your way with it. Oh...there is one last thing."

"Yes?" said Margaret.

"The city government had sent notice to the firm that the house requires demolition. The cost of demolition will require an unfortunate chunk of the monies."

Margaret drummed her fingers on the desk and then replied, "Can we stall them?"

"Possibly...I can look into for you if you like. But I would advise taking care of this sooner rather than later to avoid any violation fees that might accumulate."

Margaret took a deep breath. "I'll take that risk," she said.

Robert smiled. "I imagine you do quite well at the craps tables," he said.

"No...I leave that to my husband to pursue."

Robert did not comment on Margaret's remark and instead said, "Anyway, with our fees taken out and all the labor costs incurred in the treasure finding endeavors and securing the property...." As he talked, he pulled over a desk calculator from the corner of his desk. He referred to a typed line item list of expenditures as he rang it up on the calculator. "And that leaves a total of $28,543.00."

Margaret nodded. She had already figured the rough amount in her head and it sounded on point.

She decided to tap into Robert's mind on one more thing.

"So, Robert, by this point, I think it's a fair assumption that you have an opinion on the oddity of my aunt's situation..."

Leaning back in his chair, he said, "I have to admit to some prurient curiosity on the subject. And if I had to hazard a guess, I think the root of it could be as simple as sisterly rivalry. Maybe even involving a gentleman suitor in their younger years? Neither of them ever married I noted when I was researching the identity issue. Seems odd for the times."

"Well yes but no," Margaret replied. "You must remember that the Civil War was going on and they did reveal to me during a visit a while back that at least Blanche's beau was a casualty of war. What was his name again...oh that's right. So unusual...Blackwell Swann."

Robert tented his fingertips together. "Hmm," he said.

"What are you thinking, Robert?" She had noted his razor

sharp mind on several occasions and really wanted his take on the situation.

"Could this tie into the tunnels in any way?" he said. "Blanche's knowledge of the tunnels?"

"I couldn't say."

"I have been wondering if she went into the tunnels for some other reason than escaping Blue Plains. Could she have left something down there?"

Margaret felt a shiver. "It's all getting a little too gothic for my taste."

Robert's eyes glinted with interest behind his glasses. "Oh not for me. I love a good mystery myself."

"What are you suggesting exactly?"

"Well...what if she left some monies in the tunnels?"

Margaret pondered that for a moment before answering. "I didn't think of that...but I should have. You are right. She could have very well done that. How would we find out?"

"I think it's obvious. We have to go down into the tunnels."

"Surely you don't mean we go down there and look ourselves?"

"Do you really want to risk somebody pocketing more of the monies?" he said.

She shook her head slowly. "No. I've never been a fan of tight spaces though."

"Nor I. Look, I can hire a city engineer to help us navigate and lessen any possible danger."

"Okay, but let's back up a bit. Shouldn't we have a conversation with Blanche first and try to learn more from her?"

"We can try but she hasn't been forthcoming at all to date."

"It's worth a try if I can avoid going down into those tunnels." Margaret cringed again at the mere thought of what might be down there. Spiders, rats, smells....She didn't view herself as the simpering type but there was something about the tunnels that made her neck hairs stand on end.

"Very well then. You talk to Blanche and in the meantime I will make some calls to engineers."

Margaret stood up and brushed her skirt down. She held out her hand to Robert and said, "And thank you...Robert. Really for everything. I know you have gone above and beyond with this case."

"It's been my pleasure," Robert answered and looked directly into Margaret's eyes. "My pleasure," he said again and then released the pressure of his hand in hers.

Walking out of the offices of Stark, Wilson and Obermann into the afternoon sunshine, Margaret felt a shift had happened somehow between her and Mr. Brady...Robert...but she didn't quite understand what it meant...yet.

Again Margaret found herself picking up the phone and calling Judith that night.

Once she was connected, she said, "Judith, I want to be clear and upfront with you about this. I have been appointed the executor of Blanche's estate."

"Well of course, Mags. I've told you, I want nothing to do with all of that."

"But just so you know...it now involves a substantial amount of money that was collected from the property."

"And?"

"Well, I don't want you to feel...left out."

"Mags...I don't care about any of that. And I don't want to take care of the elderly. There, I've said it and it probably sounds horrible but I have my own life here and am quite comfortable. You know me...I'm a free spirit."

Margaret grinned. "You certainly are, Judith," she said. "You certainly are."

CHAPTER TWENTY-TWO

Blanche woke up stifling a scream as she came to her senses. Looking around, she couldn't remember where she was. Turquoise colored curtains hung jauntily at the windows, a lavender scent hung in the air.

Slowly it came to her...she was staying with the Frenchwoman. Her heart started to slow down. The woman had talked to her about all the lavender in Provence back in her homeland and the differences between the French and English varieties. The woman laid out lavender sprigs freshly cut on each resident's pillow at night. It did make for a peaceful slumber at first. But then the memories tumbled into her thoughts, invading her sleep. All in a jumble, Emily's lifeless eyes looking up at her with accusation in them. Running through the tunnels not being able to find Blackwell. Papa staring at her from the head of the dining room table, his voice steely with anger. Had he known? Had Emily told him? But she managed to wall off the worst memory of all, never letting it come into her mind. Ever.

She must have drifted off again because Madame Corot was moving quietly about the room the next time she looked around.

Lifting the shades and setting a cup of café au lait and a roll on the bedside table. She called it le petit dejeuner. A little lunch. Blanche's very rusty French came back to her sometimes while she listened to Madame Corot. It was heartening that it did.

"Bonjour, Blanche! We will have visitors this morning."

"We will?"

"Oui. Your niece. Very concerned about you. Wanting to make sure yesterday's events did not make you ill."

Blanche did not reply but thought back to her night dreams.

"Let me help you up." Madame Corot lifted Blanche using a fireman's hold to prop her up onto the pillows. Her looks were deceiving in terms of her strength.

As she fluffed up the pillows around Blanche's head, she said, "I will come back in a minute."

Blanche looked down at the tray that had been placed on her lap. She picked up the flaky roll and took a nibble. Then sipped at the coffee. She had become unused to eating over the years without Emily. But the habit was coming back to her. She felt herself drifting back off after a couple of bites.

"So tired, mademoiselle?" Madame Corot's voice chirped into her slumber. She struggled to open her eyes.

"Maybe I have Mrs. O'Keefe visit in here, eh?" Blanche attempted a shrug. In time, she heard whispering in the room. Maybe yesterday had tired her out more than she realized. The men with all the questions.

She smelled Margaret before she opened her eyes again. Margaret's scent was earthy almost masculine maybe from working around the horses. It reminded her of her brother although cigar smoke had hung from him also.

On opening her eyes, she studied the woman's face at her bedside: sharp, intelligent brown eyes, high cheekbones and a longish but elegant nose. She looked like her father. "Hello, Margaret," Blanche said.

Margaret sat at her bedside with a cup of Madame Corot's café in hand. "How are you feeling today, Aunt Blanche?"

"Tired. Quite tired indeed."

"It was a rigorous day yesterday, wasn't it?"

"Yes. Yes, it was."

Margaret hesitated and then said, "It seemed as though it brought up some memories."

"Memories? Maybe. Maybe it did."

"Anything you want to talk about?"

"No, dear. Not really."

"Well, when we left yesterday you talked about being a.... not as good as Emily. What did you mean?"

"Oh, I don't know." Blanche let out a sigh.

Margaret tried to mask the frustration she was feeling at Blanche shutting down again.

Madame Corot popped her head in. "Ça va, mesdames? Everything well? So much to talk about, n'est-ce pas?"

Margaret sensed a softening in Blanche and saw an advantage. She stopped Madame Corot from exiting the room. "Could you join us for a chat, madame?"

Madame Corot looked at Margaret with some surprise. "I can. Certainement."

Pulling over a chair, she placed it to the side opposite of Margaret's seat. She sat down with a frisson of energy. She clearly was not a woman used to sitting and doing nothing. Her hands immediately became busy, straightening out Blanche's bedcovers and fussing about the pillows.

After a short silence, Margaret said, "So have you two gotten to know each other a bit?"

"Ah, bien sûr. Of course." Madame Corot looked over at Blanche. "We talk of lots things, don't we, mademoiselle?"

Blanche nodded with a slight smile on her face.

"What have you talked about?" Margaret asked, trying for an innocent tone.

"Oh her adventures of course."

"Really? I would love to hear about the adventures."

Madame Corot looked at Blanche briefly and seemed to think it was okay to discuss further.

"Blanche told me about leaving Blue Plains and going to Georgetown through the tunnels! So brave!"

"Yes, it really is," Margaret said. "How did you get into the tunnels, Aunt Blanche? I found your hair ribbon by the grate at the end of the hill at Blue Plains."

"Yes, of course that is how I entered," Blanche replied.

Margaret prodded. "And then?"

Blanche shrugged. "I remembered the direction back home," she said.

"But...how could you remember after all these years?"

"It really hasn't been that many years, dear."

Margaret's mind tried to grapple with what that comment meant. Like Robert had said, it was like a mystery novel. If she viewed herself as the detective, she must backtrack to another line of inquiry. "So how old were you when you first started going into the tunnels?"

"Oh...young. That's when I was called Fair."

"Fair?" madame asked.

"Yes, because of my hair color you see. You probably can't tell now but it was quite golden in hue..." her voice faded away.

Margaret pressed on before losing Blanche to the memories. "So what took you down there in the beginning?"

Blanche shifted in her bed as if uncomfortable. And did not answer the question.

Madame Corot gave a tinkling laugh and said, 'It was l'amour, wasn't it, ma belle?"

Blanche's eyes looked off to the corner of the room and then she broke into a childish giggle.

"Who was it?" Madame Corot pressed.

Blanche looked up at the both of them and said, "Well, it was Blackwell of course. He was the only one for me."

"Did you and Blackwell meet in the tunnels?" Margaret asked.

Blanche nodded with a little smile on her face while Madame Corot gushed. "So romantique!"

"So then...did you continue to go to the tunnels after...after the war?"

Margaret did not want to upset Blanche by referring to Blackwell's demise but she had to pin it down. Eyes drifting off again, Blanche said in a soft voice, "Sometimes."

"Isn't it," Margaret said. "Well, horrible down there? Dirty, wet and rat infested?"

Blanche looked askance. "Oh no," she said. "It's a very special place, dear. Sometimes, I needed to go there to be with... I mean to be with the memories. Emily didn't understand. But she didn't need to know, did she?"

Margaret nodded as they took sips of coffee. Blanche was not any more forthcoming, so she asked, "You said yesterday that you didn't tell the whole truth of it. What did you mean?"

"Did I say that? I don't really remember what I meant." Blanche's fingers moved nervously on the plate.

"Yes, it seemed like you wanted to say more."

"No, I don't think so. I think I said enough. Everyone said it was enough."

"That's true but if there was something else..." Margaret let the thought dangle.

The clammed up version of Blanche was back in place. Sighing, Margaret decided to pursue the tunnels again. "So where do the tunnels go exactly?"

"All under Georgetown, and then somewhat further afield. I was most familiar with the Georgetown section."

"Really? What kind of things are down there?"

"Just...tunnels. Mostly."

"Anything else?"

"Well, the staircases to get out at different points. And the marks on the walls to tell where you are. That's it really."

"No nooks or shelfs or anything?"

Margaret realized too late she might have been too obvious. Blanche threw her a sharp look and said curtly, "No."

Margaret blundered on. "I was just wondering if there are places to hide things down there...if someone wanted to do that."

Madame Corot added to the thought. "Maybe there was a place to leave love letters with your Blackwell, mademoiselle."

Blanche looked down at her roll while picking at some of it.

"Or is there anything you might have left there?" Margaret's patience had worn down and she could no longer hold back.

Blanche looked up at Margaret with her baby blues. "What would I have left there, dear?"

"I don't know. That's why I am asking."

"The only thing down there are the memories of lost love."

"Oohh," Madame Corot said, and grabbed one of Blanche's hands.

"So if I were to go down there, I wouldn't find anything."

"I don't expect so. No...I don't expect so."

Margaret sat back in the chair and studied her aunt. Seemingly oblivious to it all. Or a devious liar. Or someone missing chunks of her mind. It was so hard to figure out. It was indeed a mystery.

All of sudden, Blanche sat straight up and looked intensely at Margaret. "What is today's date?"

"Uh...it is the twenty third of September, I believe." Margaret looked over at Madame Corot who nodded.

Blanche relaxed and lowered back down some. "Okay... there's still time then."

Margaret and Madame Corot exchanged a look. Margaret asked, "Still time for what, Aunt Blanche?"

"What?" Blanche answered.

"You just said there is still time..."

"I did? Oh, never mind. I didn't mean anything by it."

The conversation took unusual dips and turns with Aunt Blanche and Margaret couldn't help but wonder if she had always been like this. Or if it was a function of old age making it more pronounced.

Margaret remembered Keith's advice. "Get her talking about the old days. That's what will warm her up and get her talking." But Margaret was tired of hearing about the wonders of Blackwell. And it hadn't seemed to be any more illuminating or edifying than previous conversations.

After saying her goodbyes to Blanche, Madame Corot escorted her to the door. Margaret turned to her and said, "If she says anything else about the tunnels, anything at all, could you ring me?"

With a questioning expression on her face, madame asked, "What is it you think is in the tunnels?"

"I don't know. But I do intend to find out."

CHAPTER TWENTY-THREE

Their entourage had captured the attention of some neighborhood lads bored with the usual activities and looking for a diversion. They gathered around the grate in the alley along with Margaret, Robert, the engineer, and a worker.

Robert greeted Margaret and looked over her shoulder when she had arrived.

"Mr. O'Keefe?" he queried.

"Prior engagement," she responded briefly.

Robert nodded. If he thought it odd that Keith let Margaret engage in the adventure on her own, he did not let on. On the other hand, he probably had figured out Keith's dilettante ways by now.

The kids clamored in the alley. "Can we go down too?"

"Aww. Come on."

The engineer, a Mr. Holiday, threw a stern look their way and told them in no uncertain terms that it was against the law and that they would get in heat with the local coppers if they tried it.

"Now off with you then." Mr. Holiday was a fierce looking

fellow who didn't have to say it twice. They scattered off in different directions.

He reached down and unplugged the hatch, lifting it with one meaty forearm and placing it to the side. Cautionary orange cones had been set up in the alley to indicate to those walking about to stay back.

Mr. Holiday gestured to the worker to go down first. After a couple of moments he yelled up. "Nice and dry down here today."

Margaret breathed a little air out with relief at the mention of it being dry.

Robert lowered down into the tunnel next followed by Margaret. Mr. Holiday came down last.

The worker's craggy face was lit up by the lantern he held. He swung the light around the space in which they all stood with hunched over backs. Robert being the tallest hunched over the most and looked most uncomfortable in his stance.

"We'll head in the direction of the Healy Building. Keep your eyes peeled as we go," said Mr. Holiday.

The space was not like anything that Margaret could have envisioned. And it wasn't nearly as bad as she had thought. Bone dry due to lack of recent rain, she still proceeded with small gingerly steps looking carefully to and fro.

Some trash was strewn about the corners but other than that the state of the tunnels was not too horrible. The walls had black marks on them periodically. After a couple of minutes, the worker stopped and told them to hold up.

They stood in another wider section with a rung stair climbing the wall to a top hatch. "The Healy Building," he said, pointing to the hatch.

"This is where she probably spent the most time," Margaret piped up. "We need to look around here especially."

They all peered around the space as the worker shone the

light in the various corners. Margaret noticed ledges cut into the walls several feet apart.

"Look over there," she said.

Mr. Holiday's gloved hands scooped over the first ledge reaching back and then trying again.

"Nothing there," he reported. He continued to do the same with the other ledges finally stopped at one and saying, "Got something here."

He pulled it down and placed it in one gloved palm.

The light shining on it showed a skeleton key. They all stared at it saying nothing.

Finally, Robert cleared his throat and said, "Must open something down here, don't you think?" He directed his question to Mr. Holiday.

"No telling. I don't recall any keyed locks down here using that style of key but I could be missing something. It does get dark down here." He gave a toothy grin that gleamed in the lantern's light after saying the last bit.

"Let's keep going and look around as we do," Margaret suggested.

As the walk continued, Margaret became less leery of the space and, due to this, was not able to right herself when her left foot slipped in a wet, sticky something. Her left ankle turned and she felt and even thought she heard a crunch as it did so. Close enough to place a hand on the wall to the left, she could not stop from emitting a shriek of pain.

The men all stopped in their tracks and the worker hung the light in front of her making things worse by blinding her eyes. "What is it, ma'am?"

"I just wrenched my ankle pretty badly. I think...I think I need to turn back."

Robert edged to her side firmly grasping her arm.

"Don't place any weight on it. I've got you on this side."

"Let's take her out at the Healy Building exit and I'll summon a taxicab," he said to the men.

With each step more painful than the last, it became clear to Margaret that she had done some damage.

At the Healy exit, it took all three of the men to hoist her up the rung ladder. Upon reaching terra firma above, they placed her gently onto the ground. Crowding around her, Robert bent to roll up her dungarees. A baseball size bulge had taken over the space where her ankle had been. She gasped at the sight while the men hid any reaction.

"Yep. You got a good one there," Mr. Holiday observed.

The rest of the day passed in a blur for Margaret. Getting in and out of the taxi, waiting around Georgetown University hospital, and all the rest. Finally, hours later, she was dispatched out of the inner chambers of the hospital with crutches and an ice pack.

Robert was waiting for her in the lobby as the nurse brought her out on the crutches.

"Oh...did you not call Keith?"

"I tried...several times. His office said he was not available. Believe me, I made it clear that he needed to come for you."

"Well..." Margaret's head was fuzzy from the pain and the analgesic they had given her. "I guess I can..."

"I'm taking you home."

"Oh, that's a lot to ask of you. I really can figure something out."

He looked at her crutches and bandaged ankle and said wryly, "That's a tall order, Margaret. I don't mind one bit. I enjoy a nice drive out to the country. I rang ahead to your maid and told her to be expecting us."

Margaret could not really think of any way to dissuade him

and really her overwhelming need was to just get home. "Okay then," she said.

After making her clumsy way into Robert's car, she all but collapsed onto the front passenger seat.

"Is it giving you much pain?" he asked.

She nodded and then said, "But more than the pain, I feel the embarrassment of it happening. So silly of me. And I ended the expedition in the tunnel when we were getting so close…"

"Don't fret about it. I already arranged with the engineer to get back in there first thing tomorrow. And I will make sure there is no funny business if anything is found down there."

"Thank you, Robert. I really can't thank you enough, I guess, for all your help."

"Just consider me your local knight in shining armor." He looked over and gave a grin.

Did she imagine it or was it a flirtatious grin? Maybe it was the drugs for the pain she was on. And that shot they had given her. That was a doozy…

She laid her head back on the comfortable cushion of Robert's passenger seat and took in the dusky outside as night set in on their drive north. She began to drift off but jerked herself upright.

"Robert, what happened to the skeleton key?"

He looked over at her and patted his chest. "Right here in my inside pocket for safe keeping. Don't worry about it right now, Margaret."

She sighed and let herself relax back into the seat cushion. The next thing she knew, Robert was gently patting her shoulder. When she opened her eyes, he stared at her with concern.

"What happened?" she asked.

"You fell asleep on the drive home. Do you feel alright?"

She struggled to rise up into the seat and he grabbed her arm to help her. "Just stay put and I'll help you out," he said.

He had pulled his car to the front circular driveway and as she looked over the front door opened with Cassie standing in the backlit entrance, her face creased with worry.

Robert propped the crutches against the front of the car and then helped her to standing.

Cassie by this point stood next to them wringing her hands. "It looks painful it does, ma'am."

Robert and Cassie supported Margaret on either side and the unspoken decision was made to land in the drawing room and place her on the couch. Cassie flitted in and out of the room getting everything set up while Robert stood in attendance.

Margaret could barely get the words out but finally directed Cassie to get some food and drink for Robert.

"Don't you worry about me, Margaret. I just want to make sure you are okay here before I leave."

"I'm fine. Cassie will dote on me and not give me a choice about it. Please, I've kept you long enough."

Robert stood up with some reluctance and put his hat back on. Cassie walked back in with a something wrapped in parchment.

"Now here, Mr. Brady. I got you a nice ham biscuit and a mug of coffee for your trouble."

Robert gave Cassie a big grin and said, "That is mighty kind of you." Taking the items in hand, he looked at Margaret. She sensed he wanted to reach out and touch her. But he didn't.

He nodded at her instead and said, "I'll check in with you tomorrow."

She could barely summon the energy to thank him once more and then he was gone.

Propped up on her couch, Cassie ensured she was as comfortable as she could be and placed everything she needed fingertips distance from her. Before she even realized it, she drifted back to sleep.

Keith drifted in that night shortly after Margaret heard the clock strike midnight. He stopped in his tracks upon entering the drawing room.

"What is all this?" he said aloud. Margaret opened bleary eyes and saw Keith staring down at her with a stunned expression.

"You missed it Keith. Excitement in the tunnels," she said wryly. She looked down at the wrapped up blob at the end of the couch and said, "Sprained ankle."

"Well...why didn't you call me, my dove?" Keith said as he positioned himself on the chair across from Margaret.

"We tried...no one could track you down at the office."

Keith's eyes shifted to the left. "I was offsite for some time at a client meeting."

"Indeed." Margaret paused to make her displeasure known. "You seem so busy right now with this client." She placed particular emphasis on the word client. Keith looked away and did not respond.

Margaret continued. "Well, Robert helped me with everything and got me back here."

"Robert?"

"Mr. Brady."

"Oh right. Robert.... well, that's good then."

They sat silently for a moment and then Keith roused himself to say, "Can I help in anyway right now? Do you need anything?"

"No...I'm sleeping down here tonight. Too much to navigate the stairs right now."

"Of course, my love. Do you want me to stay with you?" He looked at her with concern.

And then relief when she responded. "I'll be fine...from the fumes coming off of you, I think you need a good lay-in anyway."

He grimaced. "The boys did get carried away a bit this evening. You know how it is. I had to keep up with all of them."

"Yes...I know how it is."

"Well...." Keith stood up and then leaned over to kiss Margaret softly on her forehead. "Sweet dreams, princess."

She closed her eyes and nodded. Her dreams were jumbled throughout the night and interrupted by twinges of pain. By daybreak, she gave up and attempted to sit up. The crutches were propped near her. She grabbed them and placed them in position, before raising herself up on her good ankle. Then she made the tenuous march out into the hallway. By the time she made it there, her heart was pounding and she felt wrung out. The crutches were a lot of work. She could hear Cassie bustling about in the kitchen and she slowly moved in that direction.

Halfway there, Cassie came into the hallway and said excitedly, "Lordy, ma'am. You gave me a fright. I said to myself who could be making noise out there? Did you get any sleep at all last night? Look at you...let me help you."

Cassie helped her back to the kitchen where Margaret plopped inelegantly into a kitchen chair and realized she was out of breath.

"Crutches are more work than I thought possible, Cassie."

"I know that's right," she said as she placed a cup of fresh brewed coffee in front of Margaret.

After a few sips, Margaret felt somewhat restored and began to process what she needed to do next. She pressed down on the frustration that being laid up was so vexing especially in the middle of Aunt Blanche's situation.

Even more vexing was the call she received later in the afternoon.

Robert and the men had returned to the tunnel seeking a location to use the key but had found nothing. Robert rang to report the latest and then said, "I think you need to talk with her again."

"I agree," Margaret said. "But now with this ankle...these crutches..."

"I can get you there."

"Can you?"

"How does eleven work for tomorrow?"

"That suits just fine." Her heart gave a little lift at the idea of spending most of the day with Robert. He had become Robert in her mind rather than Mr. Brady.

Keith had been lounging in the drawing room, keeping her company when the call had come in.

"What is it now, my love?"

Margaret brought him up to date on the key and its possibilities and then finished with, "So Robert is picking me up tomorrow. It's imperative I talk to Aunt Blanche right away."

"I see," Keith said. "Did you want me to take you, darling?"

She shook her head. "No it's fine. You tend to your...client... while you can." The air between them had become charged with the unspoken but Margaret was growing used to it.

CHAPTER TWENTY-FOUR

After Robert lifted the knocker a few times, Madame Corot opened the door, her face wreathed with its usual smile.

Her expression changed when she took in Margaret standing on the stoop with crutches. "Oh no! What happened?"

Margaret brushed her sprained ankle aside and told Madame Corot not to fuss. She was fine. "More importantly, how is Aunt Blanche today?'

"She is a little...a little, how do you say, upset. She is upset today. But she is out of her room. In the front chamber."

She gestured for them to walk into the house. Once inside she took them into the parlor. She trilled, "Mademoiselle, you have some visitors!" Turning back to Robert and Margaret, she said, "I will bring café."

Blanche sat in a Morris chair and looked up.

"Oh hello," she said, then looked at Margaret's crutches. "What happened, dear?'

"Just a silly accident. It's fine." Robert helped Margaret down to the couch cushion and then removed her crutches placing them against the wall.

"How gallant that he helps you like that. So nice to have a

gentleman at your service," Blanche said without guile. Robert and Margaret exchanged a brief look. "Yes, indeed," Margaret replied. It occurred to her that maybe she didn't remember Keith.

But the thought quickly left when Blanche asked where her husband was. "I haven't seen much of him lately," she said.

Margaret waved a hand vaguely in front of herself. "He's busy with clients and such..." Margaret thought it curious that Blanche was expressing interest in others for a change.

Margaret continued. "So how are you feeling today?"

"Oh, I'm fine dear. Just fine."

Her eyes darted around the room as she said this and one foot was tapping in a nervous manner on the floor. She seemed almost hyper alert as though watchful for something. Margaret began to understand Madame Corot's comment about upsetness.

She looked over at Robert who gave her a slight almost imperceptible shrug. Margaret began with, "So Aunt Blanche I had a question about the tunnels."

Blanche's fingers had been rubbing the material on her housecoat back and forth. Her fingers stopped upon hearing Margaret's query. She looked up and stared at Margaret.

"Do you remember anything that might need a skeleton key to open down there?"

In an abrupt tone, Blanche said, "You need to put that key back where you found it."

She attempted to rise up from her seat but weakly fell back into it.

Robert rose and helped her sit right.

"Whatever do you mean?'

"You need to leave things alone down there, I tell you!" Her eyes were sparking and her voice was shaking. Then she murmured to herself, "I'm running out of time, I'm running out of time," and began wringing her hands.

"What has got you so upset, Miss Magruder?" Robert's voice was kind but firm and his question hit the heart of the matter.

She looked at him and said, "I just don't ...I just don't... I think I need to lie down now."

Madame Corot walked in with a tray of coffees as Blanche spoke the words.

"Ah...shall we take café in your chamber then, mademoiselle?"

"No, no coffee. I need to lie down now."

"Bien sûr. Too much excitement, eh? I'm sure your guests understand." She gave Margaret and Robert a wink and a smile.

Margaret shook her head slightly. She wasn't having it. Blanche was not going to stonewall her once again.

"Uh, this will be quick, madame. Aunt Blanche, what is it about the tunnels?"

Blanche's face took on a mulish expression and she looked off to one side. After some silence, she turned to face Margaret and said, "Lilli Lamb said you are up to no good Margaret. Is it true?" Her blue eyes took Margaret in.

"What? Where is this coming from?"

"Oh yes, the mademoiselle did visit yesterday," Madame Corot interjected. "It did not seem a good visit afterwards."

Blanche began to talk over Madame Corot. "Emily says that girl is just out for our money. She's just out for herself. Although maybe with her looks...well anyway that's what Emily says...."

Margaret made a point of correcting Blanche before continuing the conversation. "You mean Emily used to say that, right Aunt Blanche?"

She could see confusion cloud Blanche's face, and then it

seemed to lift. "I said that already. Emily said that." Blanche shifted uncomfortably on the couch.

"Okay, well let me be clear here. I am not up to no good. We, all of us, are looking out for your best interests. And we are trying to keep you safe. That is what we are trying to do. For Lilli to suggest otherwise is just...well it's wrong."

There was a niggle of self-doubt for Margaret as she realized she was also looking out for the interests of Needham Forest, the Magruder family farm. Something that Blanche had a vested interest in whether she realized it or not. But she left that part unsaid setting the niggle aside for the moment.

Blanche sat silently and looked off to one corner.

"You can trust me on this over my father's grave," Margaret added.

Blanche giggled and Margaret shifted her eyes over to Robert. He maintained a neutral expression. Then Blanche said, "Oh Margaret. Don't get your knickers in a twist. I don't give a whit about what that silly girl says or does." She giggled again and then added, "I know you will do right by me and Emily."

"Um...but Emily..."

"What?"

"Oh nothing."

A headache had started behind Margaret's right eye and she really did not think she could continue in the inanity of the conversation much longer. As Robert and Madame Corot began making small talk with Blanche, Margaret pondered the situation. Blanche could seem so clear headed one moment but then so confused the next. What to make of it? And Lilli. Coming here trying to sabotage Margaret's position. Margaret had to think about how to handle Lilli.

She waited for a break in the conversation and then said, "We'll let you get that rest now, Aunt Blanche." Robert nodded and stood up then handed Margaret her crutches. Making their goodbyes, they left Madame Corot's, no further along in figuring out the mysteries or treasures of the tunnels.

Once outside, she turned and looked at him. "What now?"

He shook his head. "I'm out of ideas. You?"

"I've got one good idea."

"What is it?" He turned to look at her.

"How about a drink at the Willard?" she said a little nervously.

He raised an eyebrow. "Absolutely."

It comforted Margaret to know she could still go to places like the Willard. Places where she had gone with her father. The Willard sat on the corner of Fourteenth Street and Pennsylvania Avenue. Jutting out almost into Pennsylvania Avenue as if to state its importance and lay its claim on the nation's capital.

Robert managed to park his town car on the street very close to the entrance. He helped her to maneuver out and get the crutches in place and then make a slow path to the entrance of the Willard. Taking a pause to breathe, Margaret looked up at the bowed corner of the Beaux Arts building. The detail was intricate and spoke of another era.

Inside the wood paneled room all was a bustle per usual. The late morning crowd was finishing up and the lunch crowd was beginning its takeover. Margaret breathed in the smells. Cigar smoke, a citrusy tone and heavy money. The maître de walked them over the mosaic tiled floors past the heavy maroon velvet drapes and free standing green Corinthian columns to their table.

Seated by a window, she stared out at Pennsylvania Avenue and the busyness of the traffic.

Robert folded his menu closed which brought her back to the table.

"And what will be your pleasure this afternoon, Margaret?"

"My usual," she responded. "Bloody Mary and a side of eggs Benedict."

"I'll do the same then. You seem to know your way around the menu here."

"I do. That I do." Memories of her father filtered through her mind triggered not only by the place, but by the smells wafting around the room.

When her eyes focused back to present day, she found herself looking into Robert's eyes. Hazel brown in color she noted behind the glass of his wired oval frames. She had never noticed that before. She took in more: the laugh lines crinkled around his eyes, the smooth crisply shaved jaw line, and the hint of dimples in his cheeks. While conventionally good looking, it went deeper than that she suddenly realized. He was steady, solid. A presence.

He broke into her thoughts. "Why do you think Blanche was so upset this morning?" he said.

"I really don't know. Something is bothering her though. She keeps talking about how time is running out."

"Can you remember anything significant happening in your family around this time of year?"

"No...but then I'm more than a little rusty on family genealogy. I really couldn't tell you dates of births and deaths for the various family members."

"Hmm. Maybe that would be worth tracking down...if it explained her agitation."

The waiter moved his way into the table space, setting down tall glasses of Bloody Marys with a leafy stalk of celery poking out of each glass.

They paused to take sips of the liquid refreshment before

Margaret replied with, "I don't know, Robert. I really think we might be on a wild goose chase here. I mean…are we just trailing after a mentally unhinged person with no rhyme or reason to what she is doing?"

He sat back in his chair and took a moment before saying, "Maybe. Maybe we are. But on the other hand, what about the key? She knew about the key. You could tell that, right?"

"Yes. I have to agree with you there."

"So if we are able to find out what the key opens, any extra work, such as pinning down important family events, might be well worth it…."

He let the thought dangle and then continued. "So tell me about your father."

"My father?"

"Yes. You mentioned he used to bring you here."

"He did. He was a character I guess you could say."

"Does Blanche remind you of him?"

"Oh no. Not at all. In fact, it's hard for me to reconcile they came from the same place if you want to know the truth. He was…he was larger than life. I think that sums him up."

"How do you mean?"

"I'll give you an example. When he walked into this room… here at the Willard…all heads turned and men walked forward to have an audience with him. He was somebody, you know? But not because of how much money or power he had…just because of him. People wanted to be around him. Have you ever met anybody like that?"

Robert studied her before responding. "Yes…yes I have," he said.

She looked down and stirred her Bloody Mary with the celery stick. She had the funny feeling they were talking about two different things.

"Anyway, he also made something out of nothing. He built

the business at Needham Forest from the ground up. There is so much to admire in that, in my opinion."

"I agree. A lot to admire." He stared at her again with some intensity.

At that moment, they were served their platters of eggs Benedict. Margaret looked at the plate and smiled. Two English muffins with a poached egg on top of each bathed in a shimmery golden sauce, decorated with sprigs of fresh parsley. Just as she remembered.

"Why are you smiling?" Robert asked.

"It's nice to see that some things never change," she said.

"But you haven't tasted it yet."

"I don't need to. I know."

They talked while they ate about Robert's other cases at his office. He had a flair for picking out the interesting details from the dullest situation she noted. As he talked, she used the opportunity to look, really look, at him again. The more she did, the more she liked.

By the end of the meal, she had almost forgotten the ache in her ankle and got up a little too quickly. She managed to catch herself using the back of the chair. Robert was at her side in a heartbeat, placing his hand on her arm. "Watch yourself."

She smiled up at him with some chagrin. "I almost forgot about it for a moment."

He left his arm there as he helped her with the crutches. She liked the sensation. It felt right.

CHAPTER TWENTY-FIVE

Once the house settled down, Blanche lay in her bed and listened closely to Madame Corot's activities. She followed her movements through the house based on sounds alone: straightening up the front parlor, readying the dining table for the morning breakfast routine, then going into the kitchen and putting away the last of the dinner pots, pans and dishes. It was predictable. Blanche had listened for it every night. It was also comforting. Madame Corot was nothing if not comforting...a mother figure.

Finally, madame made her way up the staircase to the attic level where she lived her "other" life. The stairs made their groans and creaks as they did every night and madame retired for the evening. She had never come back downstairs after she went up...unless one of the residents yelled out for her.

Blanche could only imagine what it was like since she had never been up there. The stairs were quite steep and besides it was unspoken that it was madame's private personal space. But Blanche did envision it to be more French than even the downstairs. She was intrigued by the thought of it.

Giving it another half hour, Blanche stared at the green Big

Ben next to her on the nightstand table. When the big and little hands turned to twelve, she lifted herself upright. Her house mules were right beneath her on the side of the bed. She lowered herself down with trembling arms so that her feet slid right into them. Once fully up, she felt balance drift into her body. Then she walked into the parlor, making her movements slow to keep them quiet.

The phone desk was tucked away in the corner. She lifted the dial and said to the operator, "Rittenhouse 101." She was connected immediately to the Black and White Cab Company and said softly, "I would like a taxi. I need it to pull in the alley behind the house. Very important. It needs to pull behind the house in the alley."

"What's the address, ma'am?"

"The address?"

"Yeah..." With some impatience, the gravelly voice said, "We need the address."

Blanche glanced down and saw a piece of mail on the phone table with Madame Corot's address on the front. Squinting one eye, she read out, "1360 Thirty-Third Place."

"Got it, lady." The line disconnected.

Blanche slowly walked through the kitchen to the rear door. The bolt was pulled over and it took all her strength to pull it back. It made a thudding noise and she stopped to listen if it had woken anyone. Hearing nothing, she pulled the door open and made her way out into the night.

She floated through the backyard and down the path to the gate that led to the alley. There was a chill in the air but her housecoat provided her with enough warmth and her feet were well clod in the mules. She lifted the hook for the gate door and exited into the alley. Moonlight from a blood moon lit up the alley which looked pretty much the same as every other District alley in Blanche's opinion. They always had. Closing the door, she stood, one hand resting on the gate for support and one hand holding a small clutch. She waited patiently for the taxi whilst gazing into the night sky.

She didn't have to wait long. The taxicab's slow approach up the alley was guided by its headlights and Blanche walked out into the center. The brakes of the cab screeched. The driver lit out from the front and said, "Lady, you trying to get run over or something?"

Blanche didn't reply and let the short, swarthy fellow take her arm and help her into the taxicab. Once back in the driver's seat, the taxi driver turned to look back at Blanche. "Where we headed tonight anyways?"

Without missing a beat, Blanche replied. "1304 Thirty-Fifth Street, Georgetown."

"Yep. I know the street."

Blanche took in the cityscape as they drove down Wisconsin Avenue. The light from the blood moon cast shadows all about and there were not too many other vehicles out. Or people. She liked it like this. She and the taxi driver didn't speak during the ride. Without really realizing it, Blanche began talking to herself. Talking about what she needed to do next. It helped frame it in her mind. Put her house in order so to speak.

He pulled onto Thirty-Fifth and then double parked in front of 1304. After helping Blanche out, he lifted up his cap and scratched one side of his head. "You sure you got the right place, lady? This don't look too good."

"Young man, I've lived here all my life. This is my home. Now what is the fare of the trip?"

"Huh? Oh yeah. That'll be seventy-five."

Opening her clutch, Blanche poured its contents into her palm. All coins except for the skeleton key. She set the key, which she had found in Madame Corot's rummage drawer, back in the clutch. She sifted through the coins, sorting for the right ones. A gold piece was in the middle of the mix.

Handing it the man, she said, "Thank you for your service."

He doffed his cap and stood there in some bewilderment. Blanche stood still and waited for him to leave. Somewhat abashed, he got his taxi and drove back off into the night.

It was time for Blanche to get busy.

The old maples cast shadows as Blanche stepped into the backyard. She paused, taking in the site of her old space. She did love it so. But no time for reminiscing. She opened the gate and exited into the alley. Flatter and more open than Madame Corot's. But, still, a District alley was a District alley. After making her way to the grate, she gave it a push. It moved more easily than ever. She took her penlight out of the clutch and went down once again into the tunnels.

Margaret heard the phone ringing off in the hallway as she finished up her breakfast in her dining room at Needham Forest. She had been reviewing the meal she had shared with Robert the prior day at the Willard. She kept reviewing it over and over again in her head and knew she needed to stop. The phone ringing ceased and a minute later Cassie scurried into the dining room.

"I hate to do this, ma'am. It's that French lady. She says it's an emergency."

With Cassie's help, Margaret rose to standing and placed crutches underneath her armpits. Making her way to the phone, she swayed a little from a lightheadedness and righted herself. It would do no good to take a tumble at this juncture.

She picked up the receiver and said, "This is Margaret O'Keefe."

"Oh madame. We have such a problem. Mademoiselle

Blanche has left! I don't know how she did it. But she has left and I am so sorry..." Madame Corot's voice was shaky and close to tears.

"Calm down, madame. Let's think about this. I will call Robert...Mr. Brady...and he will go look for her."

She could barely get off the phone with Madame Corot's run-on apologies. Finally finishing the conversation, she dialed out to Robert's number.

Upon hearing his voice, she said, "Oh thank goodness. She's done it again, Robert. Blanche has pulled another escape. This time from Madame Corot's."

She could hear him blowing air out on the line.

"Okay. I'll alert the authorities. We'll find her."

"I really don't think we'll have to look farther than 1304 Thirty-Fifth Street. I'll head down to meet you at your office shortly."

"I'll wait for you here. And Margaret?"

"Yes?"

"You know you can count on me, right?"

"I know," she replied softly.

She worked her way back to the dining room with Cassie at her side. Keith had come down and was making headway into his omelet.

Upon her entry, he looked up with an inquiring expression.

"She escaped again."

He shook his head from side to side as he cut into another piece of omelet.

Sitting back down, Margaret resumed her meal. It served no good to let Cassie's delicious omelet go to waste.

Margaret had Keith drive her down into the city once again to the offices of Stark, Wilson and Obermann. Keith made halfhearted attempts at conversation but eventually gave up. Margaret was too preoccupied with Blanche's safety to give much response. Plus, she was finding Keith's comments more irritating than helpful.

Robert had coffee and pastries set out in his office and gestured for them to help themselves. If he was surprised to see Keith, he did not show it. Once Margaret was seated and crutches moved aside, she turned to face Robert. "What's the news?"

He shook his head with dismay. "Nothing as of yet...except one lead that she may have been in a taxi. I'm tracking down the company and the driver as we speak."

Margaret groaned with frustration. "What does she think she is doing? She can barely walk much less gallivant all over town."

Keith who had been strolling around the office with coffee cup in hand gazing at the artwork on the walls turned and said over his shoulder, "Can you really blame the old gal? She's trying to recapture her lost youth perhaps. The freedom..."

Margaret and Robert exchanged a quick look. Robert made his disdain for Keith's commentary known to Margaret in all but the briefest of glances.

"Well, where does that leave us?" she asked Robert.

"I was going to suggest that we drive over to Thirty-Fifth Street on the off chance that she has now surfaced there."

Keith made a show of looking at his watch. "Hmm. We are running into a bit of a time crunch now."

"We are?" Margaret asked.

"Oh I thought I mentioned it, my dear. I have a meeting with my client at one. A luncheon meeting in fact. Tedious but must be done."

"Of course. Your client. Once again."

The air in the room began to crackle with what went unsaid

and all the tension that had been mounting between Margaret and Keith.

Robert cut through it. "It's not a problem," he said, "I'll take Margaret over."

"Thanks ever so much, good chap." Keith walked over and gave Margaret a perfunctory kiss on the crown of her head. "I'll call you later, darling. Best of luck."

When he left the room, a weight seemed to leave with him.

Robert looked at Margaret and winked. "I guess it's just us two then."

She smiled and placed her coffee cup on the table. "I guess so...."

The drive through downtown took them through the history of the city. They made their way around Union Station with the Capitol jutting off in the near distance. Down Pennsylvania Avenue, they circled around the White House and eventually up to M Street.

As they made their way down M Street, a slow shift began on the streetscape reflecting the older age of the buildings they were passing. Georgetown had been the pulsing heart of the city even predating the new Capitol by fifty years or so. Now, the buildings showed their ages and some benign neglect. The streets were of cobblestone and the car ride became more jarring as Robert made the hard right from M Street onto Wisconsin Avenue. Once on Wisconsin, they passed the rag tag, quaint collection of shops, cafes and restaurants that some likened to a Parisian street scene. In short order, Thirty-Fifth Street came up on the right and Robert pulled over to an empty spot to park.

Robert helped Margaret out with the crutches and she carefully stepped along the brick-lined sidewalk to the front of 1304. She stopped and stared at the front façade. Signs had been plastered onto the front from the city government regarding the demolition that was to ensue. She wondered if Blanche would even understand the signs if she stood here and read them. It was so hard to figure out how much reality Blanche was able to grasp.

Robert cupped one of her elbows with a light touch. "Let's go around to the back," he said.

It was slow going with the crutches, but she made her way along the side of the house. The path had now been well trodden by all the various workers who had come and gone over the past month during the "recovery" time. It seemed like a lifetime ago now to Margaret. So many changes since then.

The beaten down path made it easier to enter into the maple bowered back yard. All the tin cans and other debris had been removed making it less likely to trip. Even on crutches.

Upon entering the space, Margaret and Robert immediately looked over to the back veranda. And there she sat plain as day. Blanche.

Margaret let out an "Oh!" She half wondered if she was a ghost. Robert grabbed her elbow tighter. It seemed to have unnerved him too.

Blanche gazed over at them upon hearing Margaret's utterance. She sat as though not having a care in the world in a flowered housecoat and some mules on her feet. Her hair was pulled back in its usual chignon although most of it was escaping from its knot due to God knew what activities the previous evening. Her face was weary and appeared more lined than Margaret had noted before, but they were in natural light.

"Hello," she said casually.

Margaret and Keith made their way to where Blanche was perched on an old camp chair that must have been left behind by one of the workers. They walked up onto the veranda and all three of them looked out over the yard.

Because it was early fall, the Black-eyed Susans that had infiltrated the yard were winding down and taking on the darker hues of the new season as they began their fade away. "The Black-eyed Susans really took over the yard this summer, didn't they?" Margaret said.

Blanche stared out and Margaret didn't know if she had even heard her until she spoke a bit later. "My neighbor, Melinda, gave me a clump of them a long, long time ago. See how you can take something small, just a clump, and then it blooms all over, everywhere. That is really something, don't you think so?"

She looked up at Margaret who nodded and then said, "I do. I do think so. My father used to call it English Bull's Eye."

Blanche continued as if Margaret had not spoken. "Kind of like some families. The Magruder family took off like that, didn't it? Our forbearer coming over from Scotland and so forth and so on."

"I never thought of it like that," Margaret reflected. "But I can see that. A garden of many years is like a family taking root and growing."

Blanche replied on a different note. "Melinda and I were debutantes together. She was there the night I met Blackwell..." Her tone became wistful as it always did when she spoke of Blackwell.

Margaret was too worn out to engage in any discussion about Blackwell so she lowered herself down in a camp chair next to Blanche and studied the Black-eyed Susans. There seemed no point in asking the why, where and how. She already knew she wouldn't get an answer.

The back door was ajar. "Did you go inside the house, Blanche?" Margaret asked.

"Well of course I did, dear. I don't sleep under the stars at night, you know." She gave an odd chuckle.

Robert and Margaret looked at each other and then he said, "Shall I check that everything is okay in there?"

"I can already tell you things are not okay. The thieves took all my things out. Didn't leave a stick of anything behind." She had a beleaguered look on her face but did not appear to be as upset as Margaret would have thought.

"So...you slept on the floor I guess."

"There was a blanket in the front room. I don't really know where it came from...but it served its purpose last night."

"Well..." Robert said, "I'm sure Madame Corot is worried about you. Let's lock up here and get you back to your comfortable room there."

Blanche shrugged and said, "As you wish."

Margaret and Robert were both surprised at the easy acquiescence Blanche was giving but got her moving along before she could change her mind.

Robert pulled the back door shut and used one of the keys he had on his extensive key ring to lock it. He then helped Margaret down first followed by Blanche. Margaret had the thought that she really was putting a lot on Robert. But he seemed not to mind.

It was a careful process to get back to the front and once there all three took a breather. Margaret had forgotten about the demolition notices and quickly looked over to see if Blanche was reading them. She wasn't. She stared down the street and patiently waited for Robert to do whatever was next.

Once at the car Blanche demurred at Robert helping her into the back and lithely pulled herself in. Neither Robert nor Margaret had noticed the burlap bag that Blanche had hidden underneath her house coat---the bulge it made. Now more pronounced as she sat in the back seat. They drove off back to Madame Corot's.

They made quick work of dropping Blanche off. Madame Corot was ready at the door and bundled Blanche in taking her straight back to her bedroom. She said her goodbyes over her shoulder and Margaret said she would be in touch. They headed out to the Black and White Cab Company on Connecticut Avenue that Robert had the lead on.

The lot was about half filled with taxis and a cluster of cabbies stood around the wooden booth that served as their "office". Robert helped Margaret out and she propped herself against the side of his car while he went to find someone in charge.

After some gesticulation, a small man emerged from the cluster and followed Robert over to where Margaret stood.

"Margaret, this is Mr. Clancy who has been identified as driving the cab that night."

She nodded to him. "So can you tell us again how this all happened?" Robert asked.

He took his cap off and scratched a tangled thatch of dark hair. "Well, I got a call for a pickup in an alley up in Glover Park, see?"

He looked up at both of them as if for approval. Apparently seeing whatever it was he needed, he continued. "When I got down the alley, an old lady in a nightdress was standing right in the middle. She coulda been hit you know? Anyhows, I stopped the cab right there in the middle of the alley. The headlights lit her up and she was staring right at me with big eyes. I don't mind saying it gave me the heebie jeebies."

After a brief pause, Robert encouraged him to continue. "So...did you get out of the taxi?"

"Well, yeah. Her being old and all. That's a service I do for all the elderly," he added with a measure of pride.

"And?" Margaret asked.

"I got her in and she told me where she wanted to be

dropped off. That's it. I dropped her off where she wanted me to, lady."

Margaret and Robert looked at each other and then the driver.

"Was there anything else?" Robert asked. "Anything she said? Or did?"

He stared off to a point in the taxi lot and then turned back to them. "Yeah, as a matter of fact there was. She paid me with some real old coins. I didn't know if they were even legit. But I felt sorry for her and didn't give her a hard time or nothing."

"Why did you feel sorry for her?" Margaret asked.

"Well, she was talking about her baby and how the baby died and all. She seemed real distressed over it."

"What? A baby?" Margaret said in a sharp tone.

"That's right. There ain't nothing wrong with my hearing, lady."

Robert handed the man a couple of bills and he sauntered back off to his crowd, looking back over his shoulder at them once or twice.

Margaret leaned heavily against the car, her ankle throbbing, and said, "Robert...a baby? What in the world?"

He shook his head. "I don't know what to make of it, Margaret. I really don't." He placed a hand under her elbow and said, "Here, let's get you seated and off that ankle. How about we take a coffee break?"

Margaret just nodded, numb from the latest wrinkle in the day's events.

Margaret and Robert sat across from each other in the Mayflower Coffee Shop and Grill. It was housed in one of the lower levels of the grand Mayflower Hotel that had quickly become a city institution after opening in 1925. The elegance of the place even spilled into something as mundane as a coffee shop. Margaret had become quite partial to it with its décor of paintings depicting the colonial era and its old fashioned style when lunching out in the city.

Margaret gazed over at Robert and smiled. The clatter of the diners around them---the talking, the clanging silverware and all the rest---disappeared and it was just the two of them. She shook her head slightly to get out of her reveries.

"So...more crazy ramblings on the part of Blanche or what?" she asked Robert.

"In my experience there's a kernel of truth in any of this kind of thing," he said. "The question of course is what part of it might be truth."

"Right. And how do we figure it out?"

They stared at each other and both said at the same time, "Ask her."

Margaret's eyes were still on Robert's face when she heard a familiar voice to the side of their table. "And what do we have here?"

When she looked over, there stood Lilli Lamb, all parts of her once again stuffed into an outfit too small for her figure. Her doughy face was stretched into a picture of indignation.

"Lilli? What are you doing here?" Margaret asked, taken aback.

"I'm on my lunch hour of course. But I don't think the same can be said about the two of you!" Lilli practically sputtered in anger.

"What is wrong with you?" Margaret asked in a rising tone.

"What is wrong with ME? How about you, Margaret O'Keefe? The question is, what is wrong with you? A married woman, gallivanting around town with a bachelor."

Robert began to rise up. "Uh...Miss Lamb I think..." he said.

"And you? Have you ever heard of conflict of interest by any chance? Because if you haven't, you soon will!" With that, Lilli flounced away from their table and they watched her awkward progression as she bumped into tables along the way to the front door.

Robert and Margaret looked at each other. Margaret could see Robert was trying to hold back a grin and when she saw that, she let go and laughed aloud. Her laughter was contagious and Robert soon joined in.

Margaret finally gained control of herself, still letting out a peal here or there.

"Oh...I haven't laughed so hard in years. I needed that."

"I guess you did."

"Do you think she's going to try to do something with her lawyer?"

Robert shrugged. "Let her," he said.

"You're not worried about it?"

"Nah. It's like her rolling up a piece of paper and trying to cut me with it. Let her."

With that, Margaret took up laughing again at the idea of Lilli attacking Robert with a rolled up piece of paper.

CHAPTER TWENTY-SIX

Madame Corot's black and white kitty lay curled in Blanche's lap on the sitting room sofa. She stroked the soft fur and stared down at the cat. It purred with contentment, eyes slit in half slumber. The inside of its ear was meticulously clean, so clean it had become translucent, almost pearly white, with black edging.

Blanche had studied the cat at other times, working hard on grooming all aspects of its body but especially the ears. That was some hard work she thought.

When Blanche had returned to Madame Corot's, she placed the bones in the safest place she had to do so: under her bed. She had always wanted Arabella with her. That was all she had ever wanted. Emily had not let her. But Emily had no say now. Arabella was home with Blanche finally.

Madame Corot breezed into the sitting room where Blanche had taken a seat with the cat after an extended nap. Madame tended to flit in and out of the various residents' spaces throughout the course of the day. In that way she seemed to keep everything about the place in check.

"Ah. . . I think mon petit Henri likes you, mademoiselle."

Blanche looked at her with a vague smile. Madame Corot

planted herself on the couch next to Blanche and Henri, the kitty.

"So...you are calm now, n'est-ce pas? Henri, he is good for that, eh?"

Blanche nodded, still stroking Henri's coat. "Yes," she said. "As a matter of fact, I feel quite refreshed indeed."

"Do you want to tell me what had upset you?" Madame Corot asked.

Blanche stared across the room. Then she started talking.

"Blackwell never knew. He left before I even knew. Once I did realize, I kept it a secret. But Emily figured it out. She was always clever like that."

"Emily? Your sister?"

"Yes, my big sister. So bossy. I guess all big sisters are..."

Madame Corot nodded.

"Emily kept the secret too," Blanche said. "And I needed her help when it was time."

"Time?"

"For the baby to come."

Madame Corot reared back a little in surprise and then only asked, "So she got the doctor..."

Blanche interrupted, "Oh no. There was no doctor. We had to keep the secret you see."

Madame Corot had a perplexed look on her face. "So how did you deliver..."

"Emily. Emily delivered my baby."

Raising eyebrows, Madame Corot said, "She was skilled like that?"

"No, she wasn't. That was the problem. The cord was wrapped around the neck and Emily didn't know...so..."

"Ah," Madame Corot murmured.

"There was so much blood..."

"So then Emily got you help..."

"No. We were in the tunnel room. It wasn't possible to get help."

"The baby was born in the tunnels?" Madame Corot asked with a hand to her heart.

"Yes. We had to keep the secret."

"But it must have been horrible to have a baby down there."

"Horrible?" Blanche looked blankly at Madame Corot. "Yes. I guess it was. But Emily insisted. All the noise and mess would wake up Papa and Mother, she said, if we stayed at the house."

Tears had begun to form in Blanche's eyes and her mouth moved at the corners as she tried to control her emotions.

"So..." Madame Corot prompted in a soft voice.

"Emily told me my baby was dead," Blanche said, her voice quivering. "After some time, I got up and we left her there. Just...left her there. I took to my bed for a long time. Emily told my parents that I had the influenza. She told them she would tend to me so that they wouldn't get infected. And she told me to forget about the whole thing. But I didn't. I couldn't."

The story had rendered Madame Corot motionless. There were not many things that did so. The two women sat together silently for some time. Then Madame Corot sat back on the couch cushion and began to pet Henri's fur.

Madame Corot looked out of her element in the office drawing room. Her hat was off kilter and her cheeks were flushed. Her hands positioned on top of the purse on her lap moved to and fro.

Margaret and Robert walked into the room closing the door behind them.

"Who is taking care of things at your place?" Margaret asked.

"I have someone who can help me when something important comes up that I need to attend," Madame Corot said. "This cannot wait."

She had called Robert the previous afternoon specifying that she must see him and Margaret right away the next morning. He had set things up and the three now convened.

Margaret, worried, asked, "What is it? Has Blanche become too much of a problem for you?"

"Non, non. She is not a problem like that. But there is this that she told me."

She took a pause as if gaining strength before speaking. Margaret and Robert waited for what was to come.

"She went to the tunnel to look for her baby."

"Her baby?" Margaret exclaimed. "This is the second time we have heard of a baby. What is going through her head?"

"I believe her, madame. There were so many details...." Madame Corot went on to explain about the birth and Emily's role. Robert listened, his face frozen with a shocked expression, as Margaret studied Madame Corot trying to work out what truth, if any, was in the story.

After she finished speaking, Robert said, "Okay. Look. There is a way to figure this out. If all this is true, there would be human remains somewhere down there, right?"

The two women looked at each other, both uncomfortable at the idea.

"So we will form a team to go and see what we can find," Robert said.

"You know...there was the key," Margaret said. "We never found the door for the key."

"She said there was a room," Madame Corot added. "A room where the baby was born."

"Okay, we have all the old engineer's drawings. I will get

someone on this right away. If there was ever a room, it's got to be on those drawings."

Margaret lounged in Robert's office until Mr. Holiday, the engineer whom they had worked with previously, could meet them later that afternoon. His office space included room for a nice, burgundy leather couch which allowed for plenty of room for her to elevate her legs. She gently closed her eyes as Robert took pen to paper at his desk across the room.

She didn't realize she had drifted off until she heard a door slam somewhere else in the building. Opening her eyes, she looked over to Robert's desk. He was already looking at her and he gave her a wide smile. He got up from his desk and stretched. Then he walked over and took a seat across from Margaret in the armchair.

"Feel better?" he asked.

Righting herself up to sitting position, she said, "I don't know that I should have been that tired to start with. I'm not that old yet!"

"These past couple of days have been pretty busy." He pointed to her ankle. "Plus, how is it feeling anyway?"

She took a look at her ankle. The swelling looked a little less. "I think I might be turning the corner with it, actually."

"Well," Robert said, looking at his watch. "We have time to take a small lunch here. I took the liberty of ordering some sandwiches and was waiting for you to wake up."

"Oh...you should have just woken me up. You're probably starving to death."

"You needed the rest. I didn't mind waiting. Really."

He gazed at her intently. The moment stretched and then she ended it by saying, "Well, let's see if you ordered my favorite."

"I guessed a hot turkey and Swiss?"

"Fair enough. I'm a roast beef and Swiss girl but I can handle turkey and Swiss," Margaret said with a teasing note in her voice.

She watched Robert as he deftly laid out the sandwiches and accompaniments on the table in front of them. She wondered how she had gotten so lucky as to get his attention like this, but wasn't going to complain about it.

Instead, she let the feeling of contentment wash over her as they ate their sandwiches and chatted.

Eventually, Robert said, "I hate to end this, but Holiday will be here shortly."

He wrapped all the trash up and wiped down the table readying it for the engineer's plans.

There was a knock on the door. "Come in," Robert said.

Mr. Holiday walked into the room, holding his hat in one hand and rolled-up plans underneath his armpit.

"Thank you for meeting us on such short notice, Mr. Holiday," Robert said. "It is a matter of some urgency."

"Happy to oblige, sir." He looked over at Margaret who was attempting to stand. "Please, ma'am, stay seated. How is that ankle of yours?"

"Much better than the last time I saw you, Mr. Holiday," Margaret replied. "Thank you for your concern, and for coming today. Please sit down."

Once situated around the table, Mr. Holiday pulled out the plans from the rolled-up tube and stretched them across the tabletop.

"So...I've already studied these back and forth and I see no traces of a room at all."

He placed a finger at a point. "This here is the staircase that goes up to the Healy Building. If you look either way to the left and the right of it, there is no delineation of any space for room."

Robert lifted his arms overhead as if to help him think. Margaret stared at the plan as if willing the room to pop out.

"But then...I realized something." Both Margaret and Robert stared at Mr. Holiday to hear what was next. His face crinkled into a slow smile making it lose some of its fierceness.

He reached over and pulled another plan from the tube roll.

"What's that?" Robert asked.

"This, sir, is the original plan for the tunnels." He laid it on top of the other and stretched it out. "At some point, they decided to redo the original plan to incorporate some new steam pipes. So here, take a look..."

He pointed to the Healy Building and traced his finger over to the west of the Healy Building staircase, stopping at an indentation in the tunnel wall. "This right here must be the room."

"How did we miss it when we went through? And when all of you went back through without me?" Margaret asked.

"I think the doorway might have been disguised in some manner. They did things like that back than...as a security measure."

"So the key?"

Mr. Holiday nodded. "Quite possibly that is a key to this space," he said.

Feeling a rush of excitement, Margaret looked at the men in front of her and said, "What are we waiting for?"

"Now wait a minute, Margaret. With that ankle of yours..." Robert began but Margaret interrupted him right away.

"I can do this...I need to do this. I just may need some extra help but it will be worth it."

The two men glanced at each other and Mr. Holiday shrugged. "I'm fine with it," he said. "We got you out once when you were worse off. We can do it again."

"Well..." Robert paused, letting out a sigh first, and then continued. "I surrender. When can we get back down there?"

Mr. Holiday looked at his watch and then back up at the two of them. "No time like the present I say."

Margaret looked down at her outfit, hose and a skirt with her low heels. A boiled English wool jacket in mauve tones was draped over the couch. She would leave the jacket in the car and make do with the rest of it

"Let me give you an old cardigan to wrap up in so you can cover up some and not worry about getting dirty," Robert said as he saw her examining her outfit options. She wondered if he had been reading her mind.

He pulled open a small closet behind the office door and took a dark colored cardigan from a hanger. When Margaret got to standing, he helped her to put her arms in and she felt the reassuring pressure of his touch. The faded scent of his cologne, a Bermuda spice rum scent, enveloped her as she pulled the sweater closer.

The trio made their way out of Robert's office and headed to the tunnels.

CHAPTER TWENTY-SEVEN

Margaret and Robert followed behind Mr. Holiday in his utility vehicle through the city streets, back over to Georgetown. They parked near the Healy Building on the campus of Georgetown University. A sprinkling of college students filled the walkways in front of the grand edifice that served as the University's core. The building, constructed in an ornate, medieval design, struck a dramatic note and included towers, dormers, tall chimneys and finials. Its crown jewel, however, was a handsome clock tower at the uppermost level. Stealing the clock hands was a long-standing student tradition at the University if Margaret remembered correctly.

Leaves had started to fall and danced in the wind with the change of seasons setting in. The two men supported Margaret on either side as they made their way to the Healy Building grate. As they walked, they received some curious looks from students, but most seemed oblivious to the presence of "outsiders".

After removing the grate and setting up the hazard cones, Mr. Holiday again made his way down the wall stair torch in hand. Once down, he yelled up, "All clear!"

They handed Margaret's crutches down first and then she began her descent by favoring her good leg and placing as little weight as possible on the bad ankle. Once in the tunnels, Mr. Holiday helped her with her crutches and Robert nimbly lit down in quick order.

They walked several feet to the west and then Mr. Holiday stopped. He took the torch and slowly worked it over the tunnel wall, taking his time. "Anybody see anything?"

Robert and Margaret both said no.

He switched to the other tunnel wall on the opposite side and did the same thing. Again, nothing. "I'll move just a foot or two and really take it slow," he said.

They all focused on the wall waiting for a door to pop out.

"Wait," Margaret said. She pointed down to her knee level. "Isn't that a door edge?"

"Well by golly I think you're right, ma'am."

The *door* turned out to be a half door with the top edge of the frame at waist level. Once Mr. Holiday trained the light all around it, they could see the keyhole for the skeleton key.

"Okay, who has the key?"

Robert reached into his inside jacket pocket. He moved his hand back and forth but came up empty.

"Oh no, Robert. Is it back in your office?"

He smacked his forehead lightly. "It's in my other jacket. I feel the fool."

Mr. Holiday gave a chuckle. "No worries, folks. I have a skeleton here on my key ring. It should do the trick."

"How can that be?" Margaret said.

As Mr. Holiday held the torch at his key ring to find the right one, he explained, "The thing that most folks don't realize is that it's usually one size fits all when it comes to skeleton keys."

"Well, that's a new one on me," Robert commented. "But I'm glad it's the case right now anyway."

"Ah-ha. Here it is." Mr. Holiday bent down to work the key into the lock but stopped. "Look. It's already open. See the edge of the frame is about a half inch ajar?"

"Yep, I see it," Robert said.

Mr. Holiday looked back at the both of them. "So...who is going to do the honors?"

Margaret's heart fluttered. She turned to Robert and said, "You do it."

"Are you sure?"

She nodded.

Mr. Holiday moved back a step so Robert could edge in. Robert squatted down and gained purchase of the door edge, pulling outwards. The door gave a loud groan.

Once the door was open, he stayed in a squat and all three were quiet. Margaret thought briefly how odd it was: the quiet in the tunnels with the bustling college campus right above.

Robert cleared his throat and Mr. Holiday edged forward with the torch, squatting down himself. He looked back at Margaret and said, "We'll go in first and then help you if that's alright."

Margaret said yes.

Once both men were inside the doorway, Robert reached his arms out to pull Margaret in. Awkwardly dragging her bad leg behind her, she worked her upper body through the doorway with his help. Once in, the ceiling was the same height as the tunnel and they all were able to stand.

The smell was even older and mustier inside the room than in the tunnel. Margaret thought she sniffed a faint tinge of lavender as well but cast that aside as impossibility. As Mr. Holiday worked the torch around the space, Margaret took it all in. It was about ten feet by six or so in her estimation. On the floor there was an old style straw tick mattress with more stuffing hanging out than in. A wooden crate was propped on one side next to the table.

"What's on top of the crate?" Margaret asked, pointing towards it.

Robert stepped closer to examine with Mr. Holiday holding the light.

"Huh. Looks like an old kerosene lamp. Empty of kerosene of course."

"We should probably look under and around the mattress, don't you think?" Margaret asked Robert.

He nodded and proceeded to sift through the ancient bedding materials first.

"Looks like just some stained old sheets and blankets. In pieces really. Watch out...I'm going to move it and who knows what might be underneath."

Margaret made herself thin against the door wall while Mr. Holiday moved closer with the light.

Margaret could not see anything as the men grunted with exertion to move the mattress.

"Anything there?" she finally asked.

"I'm not seeing anything really...just a chalky substance," Robert said, "Some old newspapers. No money caches yet."

"I don't think this room has seen anybody in it for years and years," Mr. Holiday piped in. "That's my guess anyway."

Robert interrupted. "Wait a minute...here is something. There's a label on the mattress...half off, but still here."

"What does it say?" Margaret asked.

He ripped it off completely and went over to where Margaret stood. Mr. Holiday held the torch above their heads. The label read, "Swann Fine Furnishings, Lynchburg, Virginia"

"You have to wonder who got a mattress down here at all," Robert said.

Margaret grabbed his arm. "Robert, don't you remember? Blanche's beau who died in the Civil War?"

"No...what about him?"

"His name was Blackwell Swann. His surname was Swann. Could this be where they met?" Margaret wondered aloud.

"But how would they have gotten down here?" Robert asked.

"Well, the same way we did I assume. And maybe he was able to drag his mattress down in the cover of darkness. Remember Blanche got so upset about the key and told us to put it back?"

"We need to verify this about Blackwell," Robert said.

"Well...here we are at Georgetown University. This is supposedly where he matriculated before being called to war. Could we go to the building where they hold records?" Margaret asked.

"Which happens to be Healy actually."

"How convenient," Margaret said wryly.

Mr. Holiday gave a cough. "You folks about done down here then?"

"I guess so. What will you do about this room now?" Robert asked.

"That's a good question. I'll run it by the big boss, see what he says. I'd hazard a guess he'll tell me to lock it back up and label a key for it in the shop." He gave a chuckle. "I mean it's not like we can use the room for anything. Must have had a purpose before the new steam pipes and then it kind of got walled off. But this all would have been years ago as you know. Anything you folks want to take with you before I close up shop?" he added.

"Just this label. I can't think of anything else," Robert replied.

"Alrighty then."

They left by crouching down again and going back through the odd half door. Mr. Holiday locked it up, jiggling the handle to work in the skeleton key. Once back at the staircase, Robert climbed up first and then Mr. Holiday positioned his arms in a fireman's lift to hoist Margaret to the surface.

She felt embarrassed by his hands embracing her lower body but tried to give no indication once they all were back at the grate.

Robert and Mr. Holiday shook hands, and Margaret thanked him once again for all his assistance. He loped off down the walkway carrying his tools with him.

Gazing after him, Robert said, "He's a nice enough guy, but hopefully we won't be entering the tunnels again with him anytime soon."

"Or entering the tunnels at all for that matter," Margaret said with a shiver.

"Let's get you inside the Healy Building to warm up."

The building stood large in front of them. Dating from 1870s, its stone construction reflected an earlier era when materials had been more abundant. Making their way up the marble stairsteps, Margaret was briefly reminded of going to Blue Plains. She gazed over at Robert and thought about how they had walked up those stairs together too. Things had definitely shifted since then...in ways she could not have predicted.

In the grand entry hall of the Healy Building, they walked forward to the receptionist desk and asked for the records room. They were directed up a sweeping staircase to the second floor. Margaret, crutches in place, felt her ankle complaining but put mind over matter. They needed to get this information. She felt like they were closing in on the truth. That it was tantalizingly close.

The clerk at the mahogany office desk looked up at them

with a questioning expression.

Robert stated what they needed and they were given a desk to use off in one corner of the room.

"Margaret, sit here and elevate that ankle. I'll go pull the records."

She sat down heavily with a sigh, her ankle throbbing as she placed it up on a chair. To distract herself from the throbbing, she took in the room around her: tall almost ceiling to floor length windows graced two sides of the room. Rich woodwork included a coffered ceiling and heavy wainscoting. The wall without windows was lined with bookshelves holding ancient volumes of unknown origins. Margaret had never been much of a reader but she imagined if she was this would be the perfect setting to do so.

The thudding of several books on the desk announced the return of Robert. "This will give us a good start," he said.

Margaret picked up one of the volumes and read the title aloud, "'Civil War Soldiers of Georgetown University, 1859-1865'. Okay...let's see if it has an index."

Moving the pages to the back of the book, Margaret found the index and paged through to the Ss.

"'Standish, Svengard, Swann'...oh, here it is! ' Swann, Blackwell, page 201'."

Robert moved in closer so they could read together. She felt his warm breath tickling her cheek, distracting her.

She fumbled a bit with the pages before finding the right one.

"It looks like they did a write up on all the officers, who he must have been," Robert commented.

Margaret and Robert began to read the excerpt and Margaret started saying some of what she considered to be the highlights out loud.

"Born on a farm in Orange County.... studying law....

distinguished himself at the Battle of the Wilderness, Blanche mentioned that to me once, and...wait...he stacked arms at Appomattox? But Blanche said he died in the Battle of the Wilderness. Oh no...."

Robert shook his head grimly. "He looks like he pulled one over on Blanche."

Margaret read the last line. "After the war, finished his degree at University of Richmond in law. Lived in that city with his wife and four children until his death in 1910."

She sat back in the chair distancing herself from the book. "That is terrible. Blanche must have never known he lived. But why did she think he died?"

Robert shook his head again saying, "I really don't know. Could her sister have..." He let the thought dangle.

"You mean Emily?"

"Yes. Some of these sister relationships really get complicated, it seems. I have noted this in clients I have had."

"How do you mean, Robert?"

"Well, there are jealousies, competitions and the like...."

Margaret placed a hand on her chin, rubbing it gently. "You know...you just may be onto something." Margaret's thoughts flitted briefly to her sister, Judith, and their relationship.

"Okay...next let's see if we can find anything else about the Swanns. How about under benefactors?"

Robert lifted up one of the other volumes. "Already pulled a book for that, too." The subtitle was "Prominent Families associated with the University".

This time, Robert checked the index and again found Swann directly.

They placed their heads close together again and read. The Swann family of Lynchburg, Virginia had sent all of their five sons over the course of the years to the University. Blackwell being the youngest and the last of the dynasty.

The family was indeed known for its stores throughout the southern tier of Virginia that specialized in fine furnishings. The store was called: "Swann Fine Furnishings, Lynchburg, Virginia".

Margaret said upon reading the store name, "Aha!" She read aloud the rest, "'The Swann family has been benefactors of this University for many years having all five of their sons attend the University. Sadly, one of these sons, Barrett, was lost at the Battle of Chancellorsville. Several of the surviving sons carry on the esteemed business of home furnishings in their native city of Lynchburg.'" The write up went on to detail each son's name and his time and accomplishments at Georgetown.

"So...is it possible that one of the sons or maybe more than one acquired that mattress and took it to the tunnels?" asked Margaret. She followed with, "And, if so, I don't think we have to take too many guesses what the mattress was intended for..."

Robert picked up on Margaret's train of thought. "It's fair to assume it all ended with the youngest and last to attend. Blackwell. And in Blackwell's case, Blanche was at least one of the ladies involved..."

Margaret spoke the thoughts going through her head aloud. "Blackwell was a cad and Blanche never knew it. Or if she did know it, she didn't let herself believe it. This story just gets sadder and sadder..."

She paused looking across the room and then continued. "And it wouldn't do any good now to tell her, would it? What would be the point? She's lived with the fantasy for so long that it became the reality."

Robert cleared his throat and said, "There's the issue with the baby...if there was a baby. Did Blanche have Blackwell Swann's baby? Or was that part of the fantasy?"

They stared at each other, neither knowing what to say or do next.

CHAPTER TWENTY-EIGHT

The next day, Margaret called Judith and waited for the hollow rings to come to life with Judith's voice. As she waited, she realized she was growing attached to these calls. In fact, she was growing attached to her.

Judith answered with grogginess in her voice.

"Oh, Margaret. What time is it?"

"Time to get up! That's what time."

"Ha! I stayed later at the Playwright's Bar than I should have...what's happening on your end?"

Margaret told Judith of Blanche's latest escape. Judith gave an appreciative whistle. "She's really something, isn't she?"

"But there was something really bad that happened to her."

After hearing about the alleged baby and her beau's callousness, Judith gasped and said, "Oh how perfectly horrid. The poor dear."

"Yes...it really is shocking."

As though she could not handle thinking about it more, Judith suddenly asked, "How is Keith these days by the way? Still running around with his 'investments'?" Margaret took note of Judith's emphasis of the word, investment, and wondered if perhaps Judith was shrewder about some things than herself.

The sisters said goodbye and now when calls ended there was the implicit underlay that another call would be soon to follow.

After the call, Margaret grabbed one crutch and made her way down to the barn despite Cassie's admonishments. Oliver yipped and yapped by her feet thinking the crutch was a game. She burst out laughing at the quizzical turn of his head when she stopped and kept the crutch still.

Getting closer to the barn, she felt grateful for her ankle healing. Her body doing what it needed to do to get her back to where she needed to be. It was always so easy to overlook things when all was right with the world...

Her thoughts turned to her many woes. She could not overlook these woes while her body was taking care of its own problems. Keith...if only...but it did no good to dwell. At least he had stopped asking for drafts. Drafts that she no longer had the ability to provide him even if she had wanted to. Which she did not.

She stopped in her tracks. It suddenly struck her as very odd. What was Keith doing for money if he wasn't getting it from her? She had been so occupied with Blanche that she had not realized this. In fact, she could not recall the last time she had seen Keith and wondered where he was. She made a mental note to ask Cassie when she returned to the house.

Finally, at the barn, she wiped some perspiration off her brow. Everything was more of an effort with the crutches. She normally did not break a sweat just walking from the house to the barn but there it was.

"Okay, Oliver. Let's keep going." He wagged in response and kept by Margaret's side.

As it was late in the afternoon the trainers had long finished.

Some horses rested in their stalls while others grazed in the paddocks. Leonard sat at the office desk with a furrowed brow staring at the ledger in front of him. He held a pencil in hand and was working figures on a separate piece of paper.

Looking up at her approach, Leonard stood up and said, "Hello, ma'am. How's that ankle doing?"

She waved it off and instead said, "Everything adding up okay?"

He cast his eyes to one side. "Never mind," she said. "I know the answer."

"Well, some of the suppliers have been making noise," he said. "But I got them back on track. Didn't Mr. O'Keefe tell you about it?"

"Mr. O'Keefe? What does he have to do with it?"

"He was down here when I came in this morning and I told him about the supplier. I just assumed..."

Margaret narrowed her eyes. "Where was he exactly, Leonard?" she asked.

He shifted in an uncomfortable manner and said, "He was coming out of the old supply room when I walked in."

"Are we keeping anything in there right now?"

"No, ma'am. Just some old miscellaneous stuff."

Margaret thought for a bit and then said, "Thank you, Leonard. Uh...why don't you take the rest of the day off? It's been a long one I'm sure."

Leonard gave a nod and gathered some papers together while Margaret sat with a little groan in the office chair, picking up a pencil and rolling it back and forth between her fingers. She waited for Leonard to make his departure. Oliver turned in a circle several times before landing neatly on the cushion in the corner of the room that served as his dog bed.

Margaret just sat for a while with the pencil moving back and forth. Then she worked her way back up to standing, feeling the effects of her recent walk. Walking back to the old supply room, she noted the door was slightly ajar. She pushed it open and stepped into the space.

Once inside the room, she worked her gaze around all the spaces which were largely unorganized and consisted of random piles. At the far top shelf on the left, however, things were stacked in a more organized fashion than the other spaces.

She lifted her chin higher and studied the assemblage of stacked equine magazines and some old cigar boxes. She grabbed a nearby chair and without giving it too much thought lifted herself up using the back of the chair and her good leg for leverage. She paused and breathed through the complaints her ankle was making.

The pile was within her reach once she caught her breath and she pushed things around. A cigar box had been pushed to the very back behind all the other things. Almost as though it had been purposely pushed away. With her fingertips, she grabbed a hold on it and pulled it towards her.

With careful movements, she got herself and the cigar box safely down and walked back to the office desk. Again sitting with relief. Opening up the box in front of her, a part of her knew what she would find.

The open top revealed a box filled with old cash like the cash she had found in the various caches around 1304. Old cash. Keith had stolen Blanche's money. But when? There had been no way for him to do so during the recovery process.

The only other spot that had not been checked after the recovery was the tunnels. Her mind raced back. She had told Keith they were expecting to find more cash in the tunnels. He must have gone down there before they went. He had found the cash before they got down there.

A swift fire of anger and betrayal swept through Margaret. No wonder he had not asked for money of late. He had done this instead. Stolen from her family. In a sense, he had been "stealing" from her for a lot of years. She had been carrying him and his debts along all this time. Enough was enough.

Her father had always warned her about men with weak chins and it had all come to pass. As she sat there in the stillness of the barn with just the office lamp light, the smell of cigar smoke slowly became stronger and stronger. She sat and breathed it in, working up energy for her next challenges.

Later that evening, Margaret heard the grating of metal on metal from the front door lock followed by the creaking of the one hundred and fifty year old door as it opened. Keith whistled a tune under his breath as he came into the foyer. Not a care in the world, she thought.

He entered the drawing room and stopped whistling upon seeing her on the couch. "Well, good evening my dear. Didn't expect you up so late."

She gave what she hoped was a neutral smile.

"Will you join me for a night cap, love?" he asked.

"Yes, I think I will."

Keith got busy mixing the drinks on the credenza that held the liquors. As he poured and mixed, he said over his shoulder in a jaunty tone, "And how are things with Aunt Blanche today?"

"Really well," Margaret answered. "So well in fact that we can move on I think."

"Move on?" he asked with his back still turned at the credenza.

"Yep. Time to take care of business around here. For a start, Leonard and I made plans to clean out the old supply room tomorrow morning."

He did a double take over his shoulder and missed a beat

before commenting. "Wonderful, my dove. Wonderful. So... tomorrow...the supply room."

"Yes," Margaret said, calmly.

Keith handed Margaret her drink and sat down on the sofa across from her.

He jiggled his own drink back and forth and only the noise of the ice hitting the glass was in the room.

As the silence lengthened, Margaret said, "You're quiet tonight."

He looked up and gave a weak chuckle. "A lot on my mind, I guess...You know, I think I could use some fresh air. Been cooped up all day. Don't wait for me to go up, my love."

"Of course, Keith. Enjoy the night air."

When Keith left the room, Margaret remained seated with a Cheshire cat grin on her face. She pulled her horse breeding magazine back onto her lap and tried to focus on the words in front of her, waiting for what was next.

Lilli walked into Madame Corot's drawing room with some determination on her face. As she walked in, she pulled down on her skirt slightly before sitting down.

She looked directly at Blanche and said, "Well, Aunt Blanche, you are looking fit as ever!"

Blanche cast a slight smile her way and replied, "So are you, dear."

Lilli fiddled with her hands in her lap before saying, "I hear you had an adventure the other night."

"An adventure? I'm too old for adventures. You know that."

"But I hear you made it back to 1304 Thirty-Fifth."

Blanche blinked her baby blues slowly, in an owl like fashion.

Lilli continued. "And how did you find it?"

Blanche looked off to the side and then said, "It's just not the same, dear. You would hate to see it now..."

"Were you looking for something in particular?"

"No. I have everything I need."

Lilli pressed on. "But it must bring back a lot of memories."

Blanche again looked at Lilli and said, "Memories? Yes, I guess it does, dear."

In fact, Blanche had been thinking about Emily more so than usual that day. Maybe going back had made her dwell on it. Dwell on that awful day when Emily had fallen and hit her head.

Blanche had blocked out the worst of it. But it had started intruding on her thoughts more and more these days. Especially the lies. The lies Emily had told.

She heard the sharpness of Emily's bitter tongue when she said, "Blackwell never came back for you. He lived through the war. It was his brother who died not him."

Her world spun on its axis and she barely got the words out. "Didn't come back? He's alive?"

Again, the acid in Emily's voice. "He never loved you, Blanche. I tried to make you see it. I finally had to tell you he died. There was no other way."

That was what drove Blanche to pull her arm back and with a force she didn't even know she had to strike Emily down. All the lies, lies, lies. The only truth in her whole life had been her baby.

But...did Emily lie about her baby being dead? She stood over Emily who was softly moaning on her father's Southern pine flooring and yelled with rage, "What else have you lied about Emily? Was my baby alive? Did you kill my baby?"

Emily tossed her head back and forth and said weakly, "I would never hurt a child. I would never do that. You know me."

"I don't know you. Did you kill her?"

Blanche's face was against Emily's so she could her Emily's whisper. "She would have made life too hard, Blanche."

At that veiled admission of guilt, a guttural sound tore on its own from Blanche's being. A sound she didn't even recognize as she hit Emily again.

Then Emily was still.

"No, Emily. No. Don't die on me!"

But Emily did die and Blanche really didn't know what was true and what were lies anymore.

Lilli Lamb still sat in front of her with questions in her eyes. Always Lilli had sat with the questions in her eyes.

"What about Emily, Aunt Blanche? What are you saying?"

Blanche realized she must have murmured Emily's name.

She came out in a stronger voice and said, "Emily was evil."

Lilli reeled back as if she had been struck. "Evil?"

"Yes, she was."

Lilli sat with a perplexed expression and said, "But the two of you were so close. Like peas in a pod I always thought."

"Ha! We were nothing alike," Blanche said.

"Well you always looked alike, that's for certain. Your hairdos and your clothing, you know."

Blanche lifted herself up higher and, shaking her finger, said, "I'll have you know missy that I was known throughout town as 'Fair, The Golden Hair'. Emily couldn't hold a candle to me."

Lilli sat back with a stunned look on her face.

Blanche continued. "She was jealous is what she was.

Mainly jealous that I captured the heart of someone like Blackwell."

Then she drew silent.

Lilli fidgeted with her clutch, revealing her impatience. Subtlety had never been her strong suit and she finally voiced the reason for her visit. "So...Aunt Blanche. You know me. I hate to tell tales on others. But at this point I have to." She paused for dramatic effect and then said, "It's Margaret."

Blanche remained silent. As silence lengthened, Blanche began to hum and then fiddle with her hair.

"Aunt Blanche? Did you hear me? I said..."

"Margaret. What about her?"

Lilli took a big sigh. "Margaret and her lawyer are...Well, there's no way to say it politely...they are in a dalliance with each other," she said.

Blanche shrugged.

Lilli pressed on, her tone becoming more agitated. "Don't you see what a conflict of interest this is for your estate?"

"No...no...not really."

Lilli's voice became louder. "You can't have the lawyer making moo moo eyes at the guardian. Your interests are in jeopardy, Aunt Blanche."

"Oh fiddle faddle, Lilli. I don't care at all. Let Margaret have some fun. Anybody can see the spark she has with that fellow. I say why not?"

Lilli was stunned again into silence, her mouth hanging slightly open.

"Close your mouth, dear," Blanche added. "It's not very attractive to have it dangling open like that."

Lilli quickly closed her mouth and stood up abruptly at the same time.

"Of all the nerve..."

Blanche looked up at Lilli and said, "I'm tired now. You can go."

"Oh I will go and...and...I don't know when I'll be back!" Lilli sputtered out.

"As you like, dear."

Lilli bustled out of the room and Blanche could hear murmurings between her and Madame Corot in the hallway. Lilli's voice, high and strident, and Madame Corot's, soft and placating.

The front door slammed and then Madame Corot came into the room.

"Ah mademoiselle. A difficult visit, n'est-ce pas?"

"Not really. Actually long overdue. That girl has never had our best interests at heart. Only her own."

"Our?"

"Emily and mine, I mean."

Madame Corot nodded.

"But she did get the truth out of me about Emily today I have to admit," Blanche continued.

"What's that truth?"

"Emily was evil."

Twenty minutes or so after Keith had left for his walk, the door crashed open. Margaret cringed at the abuse of the old door, an antique itself really.

Keith stormed into the room with Robert close at his heels. Oliver slinked in behind the two men with his tail between his legs.

"Hello gentlemen. Funny to see you both here," Margaret said in a dry tone.

"Very humorous."

Margaret looked at Keith with mock surprise on her face. "Why, whatever do you mean?"

"You set me up. Your own husband." Such ugliness in his voice.

Margaret turned towards Robert. "Thank you, Robert. Do I assume my suspicions were correct and you found Keith in the supply room rooting around for a cigar box?"

Robert nodded with his hands in his pockets looking somewhat uncomfortable.

"Are you proud of yourself, Margaret? Getting your...your... I don't know what he is to you now...getting him to do your dirty work?" Keith asked.

"Robert does need to receive the money, Keith. No matter how it is acquired. The dirty work was you sneaking off to the tunnels and stealing the last of the Magruder money, wasn't it? When it was my job to safeguard the Magruder interests!"

"I didn't...I don't..."

"Come on, Keith. You're not a child...please stop acting like one! You stole the money. Just admit it."

Keith had no response other than to march out of the room. They could hear his progress stomping up the stairs. Margaret winced again at the abuse of the house, this time, the one hundred and fifty year old staircase that groaned in complaint.

She turned to Robert and gestured to a spot next to her on the sofa saying, "Sit..."

He did so and they looked at each other. She broke the silence. "I don't know what he is going to do for money now."

"Don't make it your concern anymore..." he replied.

She nodded. "I guess I need to take the next steps whatever they may be."

Robert reached over and grabbed her hand. "I can help you."

She smiled at him.

They soon heard Keith making his way back down the stairs, something knocking against the staircase as he came down. Margaret assumed it was a suitcase. He did not stop by the doorway where they sat; instead, he walked out the front door, slamming it behind him.

CHAPTER TWENTY-NINE

The following day, Margaret awoke and looked over to see the empty spot next to her. Keith. She took inventory of how it felt to not have him there. She realized the overriding feeling was one of relief. If asked if she mourned the absence of Keith, Margaret would be lying if she said yes. In time, she assumed other feelings might come into play. But, for now, it was just relief.

Also, she felt like she could get on with it. The final tally had been documented and she would soon be able to set things to rights at Needham Forest. She owed that to her father. Owed him much more than that but at a minimum she needed to keep his business afloat.

Stretching up to a seated position, she tentatively wiggled her ankle. Better. It felt better. The day yawned ahead of her and for the first time in a long time there was nothing pressing her with Blanche's affairs. Just sitting down with the ledger books.

She thought about what it was she wanted to do with her day and realized: she wanted to visit Blanche.

She pressed Leonard into service to drive her into the city.

He had errands he could run while waiting for her visit to end. Along the drive, she thought back to the phone call she had taken from Lilli Lamb the previous evening. Lilli had visited Blanche and had declared to Margaret in a complaining whine that Blanche was "not right in the head at all".

She recalled Lilli's words. "She called her very own sister 'evil'. Who does that?" Surprisingly, Lilli ended the conversation in an un-Lilli like fashion saying, "I don't think there is much I have left to offer with this. Maybe I don't have much to offer Blanche either. When it comes right down to it." To Margaret, it smacked of a poor loser mentality since Lilli's "winnings" had been less than satisfactory. Lilli finally showing her true colors and her real intentions towards Blanche.

Upon arriving at the house, Madame Corot gave her the customary greeting of bisous on each cheek and ushered her in. "Oh what a fine chapeau," she said, taking Margaret's felt fedora with the jaunty feather on one side from her to hang up.

"Merci," Margaret said. "How is she today?"

Looking at Margaret with concern in her eyes, she said, "I get worried about the mademoiselle. She seems—eh—how do you say, less energy since her last adventure out."

"Hmm. Do you think she could be getting sick?"

Madame Corot shrugged her shoulders. "Je ne sais pas. With the elderly, it can be hard to predict, eh?"

She and Margaret walked to the sunroom off the rear of the house. Madame used it as a day room for the residents. It overlooked the neighborhood called the Palisades that consisted of sections of woods from Rock Creek Park. With the trees thinning out from the fall weather, there was more to see.

Blanche sat in a chair looking out the large paned windows. Margaret came from behind and pressed gently on her bony shoulders with both hands. "Hello Aunt Blanche."

Once she was in front of her, Blanche said, "I was enjoying

the view here. It's so refreshing to be above the trees. At my house, we were somewhat on low land.... not that I don't miss it, mind you."

"Yes, it is a different landscape here."

Madame walked in with a carafe of café. "Margaret, you will pour?"

Margaret nodded and thanked her. "Café, Aunt Blanche?"

"Oh no dear. I've had a cup already. You go ahead."

They sat together but did not talk while Margaret took in some appreciative sips of Madame's café.

Blanche eventually looked at Margaret and asked, "What brings you by today, dear?"

"Just to visit with you. Oh, and I also got you something."

Blanche's eyes lit up as Margaret rifled through her handbag and pulled out a small package. She handed it to Blanche.

Blanche took off the wrapping to reveal a package of blue satin ribbons. She inhaled sharply. "Oh how thoughtful of you, Margaret," she said. She fingered them and then looked up. "You know, families oftentimes really don't know each other, do they?"

"How do you mean?" Margaret asked.

"Well...even though we're related, we are really strangers, you and I. I remember being so happy when your father told me of your birth...and what they named you. But then time marched on and..."

Blanche's voice drifted off and Margaret replied. "We aren't strangers anymore, Aunt Blanche. And we can keep it that way from here out."

"Maybe. Maybe we can," Blanche replied holding up the ribbons in her hand as part of her response. "Are you going to ask me about the tunnels again?"

Margaret smiled. "No. I wasn't planning on it," she said.

"Good. Why don't we talk about you for a change?"

"Me? What do you want to know?"

"Where's that husband of yours? I haven't seen him lately. Just the other one, the boyfriend."

Margaret held back visible reaction to the boyfriend comment.

"Keith, he's made some bad choices, I discovered."

Blanche raised her eyebrows and looked with curiosity. "In some ways, that husband of yours reminds me of Blackwell...and look how that turned out."

"Um...how did that turn out?"

"I thought he died. But he didn't. He hoodwinked me, Margaret. And I lived my whole life based on that. There was one good thing that came of it...but it didn't last."

"I'm sorry, Aunt Blanche." Margaret grabbed hold of her hands. The look of sorrow on Blanche's face was heart rending.

"I'm sorry too. Don't let it happen to you. Do me that favor."

"I won't. You have my word. There is one thing I wanted to let you know, Aunt Blanche. We recovered all the treasure that you... stored."

"But you never found the real treasure. And you won't for a while longer."

"Are you sure you don't want to tell me, or somebody else, about it?"

"No, no. I don't need to talk anymore about it. Maybe some other time." Blanche looked at Margaret with clear eyes and an intense stare. "You know, Margaret," she added. "You remind me of myself, sometimes."

"I take that as a compliment. Thank you for saying so."

The two women sat in companionable silence and watched the unchanging scenery out the window in front of them. Content to just be.

Later, Margaret ran the currycomb across the horse's shiny black coat, back and forth in a rhythm. She had her bad ankle propped against a short stool for leverage. The action of grooming the horse did what she wanted it to: settled her mind. The stable was quiet with the exception of the horse's occasional snorts.

When a voice from behind her spoke, she halfway thought she imagined it. "Cassie said I might find you down here."

She finished the running the comb across the horse's body in the direction of the hair before turning to face him.

"You found me." She gave him a full smile. "Do you mind if I finish this while we talk?"

"Not at all. I like watching. How did your visit with Blanche go?"

"Good. It was a good visit." She hesitated with the comb. "She said that Keith reminds her of Blackwell."

"What?" Robert said with some surprise.

"Yes...she knew Blackwell was a cad after all. I guess she had just entertained delusions about him all these years. Maybe she couldn't stand to have the memories...corrupted."

"Corrupted memories," Robert said. "All of us probably end up with corrupted memories about something, don't you think?"

Margaret's mind went to Keith. All those years and times together that they had shared...were they now all corrupted for her? Maybe it was too soon to tell...

Then she looked at Robert. She suspected he too had corrupted memories about someone. And when he was ready he would share those...or not.

"Well maybe what matters is what we end up doing with them," Margaret said.

"Here..." she tossed Robert her comb and he helped her clean up the tools. They walked back to the house together.

CHAPTER THIRTY

Madame Corot had prepared a fine French meal for their supper. All of the residents had oohed and aahed over the dish, coq au vin. Indeed it had tasted wonderful to Blanche too but later the richness of it had not sat well.

As she lay in bed in the lavender scented room twisting a little each way to relieve the stomach discomfort, she thought back to the conversation at dinner. The other residents had filtered out and it had been just her and Madame Corot.

Madame Corot had asked her about Arabella again. Or had she? Had Blanche brought up Arabella? She remembered talking about Emily too. Had she told the French woman too much again? But what did it really matter anymore? Everyone was always so curious now about her doings but really her life wasn't so strange or different than anyone else's.

Madame had asked about Emily and the money. And Blanche had answered, "I kept my promise to Emily. I did everything she told me to. I hid all the money just like she told me to. She said if I did that then I could visit with Arabella again..."

Then she had let another secret slip out, whatever she saw

on Madame's face encouraging her to do so. "Emily didn't know it but I went back to visit her quite often, my Arabella." She had smiled a cheeky smile at the thought of pulling one over on Emily, remembering the delight she had always felt sneaking back into the house after being in the tunnels.

"Then, of course, I had to go back the other night. Because it was her birthday. Her sixty-fifth birthday. A very big one. I just couldn't miss it." Madame Corot had nodded. There were only so many secrets that her brain could hold in. They had been seeping out. She knew it, but could not control it anymore.

Blanche curled into a careful ball and turned to one side. The pains began to lift and she drifted off to slumber. Before falling completely, she had the sensation of a little hand grabbing hold of her free hand and a pressure fitting into the cocoon she had made. The little hand fit so comfortably into hers and was so warm. A feeling of peace like she had never known swept through her entire being. It was all she had ever wanted really.

The next morning, Madame Corot tapped gently on the bedroom door and then opened it.

"Mademoiselle? Bonjour!" she said softly in her sing-songy, accented voice.

She made her way around the room lifting the shades and allowing the sun to stream in while she waited for Blanche to begin stirring in the bed. But Blanche did not stir.

"Blanche? Bonjour, bonjour." She walked over to the bedside and looked down at Blanche who lay there with a serene expression on her still face almost as if the years had peeled off in the night. Madame knew even before she placed her fingers on the tissue-soft skin of Blanche's wrist.

It was later that day when Madame Corot was clearing and airing the room that she found the burlap bag under the bed. As anyone would, she opened the bag and found the collection of fragile, small bones within. Tears rolled down her round cheeks at the sight.

Margaret sat at the table surrounded by the attorneys of Stark, Wilson and Obermann once again. Robert sat directly to her right and even though they were not physically touching she felt like they were.

Mr. Stark led the proceedings as he had that day that seemed forever ago when he had laid out the situation at the Magruder house. Now it was a different story.

"First off, Mrs. O'Keefe, deepest condolences to you and your family on the death of Miss Magruder. A terrible thing to be sure."

Mr. Stark cleared his throat before continuing.

"We, of course, had already resolved the monies collected during the receiving process and had settled that into an account. Now that account gets turned over to you in its entirety and we will prepare the paperwork as such for signatures."

Margaret nodded. She realized she should feel elation but instead she just felt...flat. This was what she had wanted but she now wished she and Blanche had had more time. When Margaret got the call, a feeling of loss struck her to the core. Not news she was prepared for even though she knew Blanche was fragile. This aunt she had never really known but grew to know in a certain sense over the past several months was now lost to her forever.

"Now...what remains is the matter of the burial," Mr. Stark said.

"Of course. I authorize any expenses necessary," Margaret said.

"Yes...but there was, how shall I say, an unusual finding."

Margaret looked at him. She wondered how things could become even more unusual than they already were.

Mr. Stark nodded over to Robert. "Mr. Brady will update us," he said.

Margaret turned towards Robert with a question on her face. Had he left something out?

"Mar...uh Mrs. O'Keefe." He hesitated sipping a breath in. "Madame Corot was cleaning out Blanche's room and found something."

"Was it more money? The money we thought she left in the tunnels?"

He shook his head. "No, not that."

"Well?" She wondered why Robert was having such a time getting it out.

"It was...it was...bones. Little bones in a burlap bag. Bones like that of a small human. A baby."

Margaret couldn't stop the gasp that she released.

He looked at her and she knew he wanted to reach over and hold her but he didn't. He couldn't. Not yet.

"So the bones...the doctor who examined the bones said they indicated an early birth. A premature birth. Premature to the point of not survivable outside the mother's womb."

"That means?"

"It means that there was no way the baby would have survived despite any of the conditions."

Margaret gazed out beyond the board room table, beyond the men sitting with their uncomfortable expressions and out into the city. "There are so many questions that will never get answered," she said softly.

She looked back at all of them. "And really the biggest question is still why did she feel she had to hide all of the money?"

"Well, now that you bring it up, it turns out that Madame

Corot and Blanche had one last conversation the night before she died."

"And?" Margaret looked at Robert sharply. "Did she say why?"

"As you know the closest answers from Blanche tended to be roundabout ones. So she told Madame Corot that if she hid the money Emily would 'let her' take the baby's body out of the tunnel. And she called the baby Arabella."

Margaret sat stunned for a moment and then said, "But this was all in her head of course?"

"We can assume...unless Emily really did have that control of Blanche even from the grave. The competency test did result in her being classified as *non compos mentis*."

"I guess we could chalk this up to the fine line between reality and fantasy then," Mr. Stark said.

"Maybe there is a fine line for all of us," Margaret mused.

There was an awkward chuckle from Mr. Stark and others around the table in response. "Or maybe merely a function of age, my dear," added Mr. Stark.

"Well...I guess that's it then. . ." Margaret leaned on the table to support her ankle as she rose.

"Uh...there is one more thing."

Margaret didn't know how much more she could take.

All the men stood and waited for Robert to speak.

"There were notes left with the bones."

"Notes?"

"Yes...you can take them with you. And then...decide on the burial proceedings."

Robert handed over a large manila envelope clasped with string on the back.

"Have you read them?"

"Yes...yes. It's something you may want to do on your own."

Margaret understood that Robert was giving her this space

so that she wouldn't have to read whatever was in the envelope in the presence of the other attorneys. She made her goodbyes and headed back home.

Back at Needham Forest, Cassie brought her a cup of tea and a piece of oatmeal molasses bread. Margaret propped up her foot and soaked up the quiet. The peace.

She reached for the envelope. Hesitant at first, she finally spilled out its contents on the coffee table in front of her.

A smaller business sized white envelope was addressed to Margaret O'Keefe in spidery handwriting.

Margaret opened it up and read.

Herein are the remains of Arabella Magruder. Born and died on October 1, 1864, in Georgetown, District of Columbia.

Then she picked up a loose, yellowed piece of paper, tattered and torn, with faded elegant script.

I cannot help but dream of thee
All through the silent hours of night
Your laughing eyes, your spirit free,
Your voice the language of delight

It was signed *Your Valentine.*

She placed both items carefully down and the coffee table. Then she broke down and cried for all of it. All of it for which she had never cried before.

She called Judith's number later when she felt more able.

"So..." she began.

"So..." Judith parroted back.

Then it all came out in a torrent from Margaret, her last visit with Blanche, getting the call about her death and then later finding out about Arabella.

When Margaret drew silent, Judith said softly, "I feel like we were just getting to really know her."

"That's it, Judith. That's just it."

"I'm coming down for the funeral. When is it?"

"You are? Oh that would be wonderful. I would...well it would be wonderful."

"It's been too long, Mags, and time...well, time can get away from us, can't it?"

"Yes, it certainly can."

CHAPTER THIRTY-ONE

At the Oak Hill Cemetery which bordered Rock Creek Park, they formed a small group: Madame Corot, Lilli, Robert, Judith and Margaret, along with the priest. Nathaniel Magruder had purchased a section in the picturesque cemetery in the center of Georgetown back in the late 1800s ensuring that a large number of his progeny, if not all, would have a space to be buried. The day was dark and gloomy. November made it clear that winter was settling in like it does. The tree line that sheltered the cemetery along the park was bereft of leaves offering less shelter than usual.

There was only one coffin. Margaret had insisted that Arabella's remains be buried with Blanche. It was the very least she could insist upon, Blanche's wish that they be together forever. Not an ordinary request, it nonetheless was granted probably due to the unusual circumstances. Margaret also made a sizeable donation to the Oak Hill Cemetery Foundation in Blanche's and Arabella's memory. That probably helped.

She had ordered the headstone to be engraved with *Here lie Blanche Magruder and her beloved daughter, Arabella. Rest in peace.*

As the Episcopal priest read the final prayers over the coffin, Lilli sniffled loudly and Madame Corot held a handkerchief to her nose. Judith with her colorful blue velvet caftan and rich brocade fabric dress stood still as statue. Robert had surreptitiously grabbed Margaret's hand and held it. The sexton placed shovels of dirt atop the open grave and their little crowd began to make their way out of the cemetery. Robert took Margaret by one arm but she stopped him and said, "I'm just going to take a minute."

He looked at her with concern. "Are you sure?" he said. She nodded and gave a little smile. "I'll only be a minute. I'll meet you at the car when I'm finished."

As she walked back to where Blanche and Arabella were now located, Judith fell into step with her. They stopped and regarded the spot with the old Gothic chapel, the Renwick Chapel, standing sentry in the backdrop. Blanche now had the only treasure she ever had needed. And they were safe and sound together at last.

Other Magruder family members clustered nearby. Margaret first looked at Emily's stone. It was already showing signs of lichen built up around the edges. She shook her head at the thought of Emily and Blanche and the complications between them. And she looked at Judith and wondered if she was thinking the same.

Her grandparents, Nathaniel and Louisa, had a large obelisk style monument that served for both of them. Margaret ran her hand over the lettering etched into the stone that gave their names and dates.

Finally the sisters stood together in front of their father and mother's shared stone. Margaret's thoughts ran through everything quickly but most of all she hoped that she was living up to what they would have wanted. She wiped a tear away and then placed one hand on top of the stone. Judith did the same.

Taking in a deep breath, Margaret caught it midway with the realization that there again was a waft of cigar smoke in the air. Again her imagination...or was it?

Margaret linked arms with Judith and turned away from the stone and all the memories, picking her way through all the other stones in the cemetery and headed back to Robert and everything else that waited for her.

AUTHOR'S NOTE

THE SPINSTER'S FORTUNE is a work of fiction inspired by actual events that took place in Georgetown, Washington, D.C., in 1929. The events were so unusual that they became national news for over a month and were highlighted in newspapers around the country. Readers could follow the developing story of hidden treasure being uncovered in a forgotten house in an iconic neighborhood of the nation's capital.

I was led to this story by another story as so often happens in life. On the hunt for genealogical nuggets about my late grandfather, a lawyer in D.C. (who I never met but, like many forebearers, was a background influence in my life), I had been digging through newspaper articles from the time period early in his career. He was involved in the Blanche Magruder case and his photograph was included in one of the articles. Which, of course, led me to read everything I could find about the real life Blanche Magruder and her fantastical tale. Inspiration struck from that point on.

In totality, there were many conflicting pieces of information and so, fiction being fiction, I chose the aspects that worked for the novel with generous liberties being taken. The basis of the story is a fact: a spinster hiding treasure in odd places in her house before being taken away to an institution. I also incorporated the location, dates and some original Magruder family names for the basic framework of the story. Aside from that, facts and fiction separate and the rest of the tale has been spun off by my imagination especially the inner workings of the two protagonists, Margaret and Blanche, and their motivations, hopes and desires.

ACKNOWLEDGMENTS

A mountain of people have held me up from underneath allowing me to rise to this point: being published. If I think about it too hard, I would probably need to thank every single being I have ever interacted with for being stepping stones on the path. Instead, here are a few to be highlighted:

My two beta readers, Dart Clancy and Nigel Lavin, who are really a good cop/bad cop duo. Former English majors, they have both worked so hard at getting my writing in ship-shape order and have suffered to varying degrees along the way. (We did it guys!)

The former publishing company, Darkstroke, who gave *The Spinster's Fortune* its first chance as a published novel for which I am forever grateful. Bloodhound Books: who are now the novel's new home in this second edition, I couldn't be more impressed with their whip-smart team and publishing savvy and I am a lucky writer to be in their "kennel".

My terrific family who keep me hopping and keep me laughing in equal measures.

Lastly, I thank you, dear reader, for deciding to take this fictional journey with me.

ABOUT THE AUTHOR

Mary Kendall lived in old (and haunted) houses growing up which sparked a life-long interest in history and story-telling. She earned degrees in history related fields and worked as an historian for many years. Her fiction writing is heavily influenced by the past which she believes is never really dead and buried.

Fueled by black coffee and a possible sprinkling of Celtic fairy dust, she tends to find inspiration in odd places and sometimes while kneading bread dough.

The author currently resides in Maryland with her family (husband, three kids, barn cat and the occasional backyard hen) who put up with her mad scribbling at inconvenient hours.

A NOTE FROM THE PUBLISHER

Thank you for reading this book. If you enjoyed it please do consider leaving a review on Amazon to help others find it too.

We hate typos. All of our books have been rigorously edited and proofread, but sometimes mistakes do slip through. If you have spotted a typo, please do let us know and we can get it amended within hours.

info@bloodhoundbooks.com